Every Shot Counts

Navigating Life's Fairways and Bunkers to Create Fulfillment

Kevin Donoher

Below are some sources referenced throughout the text, identified by the page number on which they appear in this book.

Page 67–68: Steve Jobs, "You've Got to Find What You Love," Stanford commencement address, Stanford University, June 12, 2005, https://news.stanford.edu/2005/06/14/jobs-061505/.

Page 93: Ralph Waldo Emerson, Essays: First Series (James Munroe and Company, 1841).

Page 94: Paraphrased from Jim Harbaugh according to Omar Navarro, "Jim Harbaugh Full Transcript: Introductory Press Conference," Chargers.com, February 1, 2024, https://www.chargers.com/news/jim-harbaugh-chargers-full-transcript-first-press-conference.

Page 96: Al Pacino in Any Given Sunday, directed by Oliver Stone, Warner Bros., 1999.

Page 98: Frank Bettger, How I Raised Myself from Failure to Success in Selling (Harper & Brothers, 1947), 45.

ISBN (paperback): 978-1-962280-62-4

ISBN (ebook): 978-1-962280-63-1

Every Shot Counts is dedicated to all the family and friends that have made such a profound impact on my life. First and foremost to my wife Sarah, thank you for all the support and belief in me to achieve a life-long dream of writing a book that aligns with how I strive to live my life. This book was written when we were first-time parents and were going through a lot of uncertainty during that season of life. My goal is to live out the principles and mindset mantras in this book to always be the best version of myself for you and our family. Thank you for being the rock of our family and all that you do!

To my sons Michael and Kaiden, life isn't going to be easy. Some holes will be easier than others, and there will always be challenges along your path. Just know that I will always believe in you and you can do anything you set your mind to. And if you can apply the teachings in this book, I know you will have lived a life of great meaning and impact!

To my parents Paul and Michele, and my sister Shannon, thank you for being such an incredible family through it all. We are such a tight-knit family, and all the experiences and moments we have shared helped shape me into the man I am today.

To my friends and all those who have positively impacted my life, thank you! The greatest thing we can have in life is deep relationships, and I am so blessed and honored to have come across so many amazing people in my life. I hope this book impacts you as much as you have impacted me.

Finally, to Paulo Coelho and Jon Gordon, your two books, *The Alchemist* and *The Energy Bus* respectively, were the ultimate inspiration for me to write a similar fable on my own. Both of your books changed my life in the seasons I read them and gave me direction in their own unique ways when I most needed it. If *Every Shot Counts* can just impact one life like your respective creations impacted mine, then it was all worth it!

Table of Contents

Chapter 1

The Collapse

Beep, beep, beep!

Jack blearily reached for his phone on the nightstand, punching at it until he succeeded in shutting off his morning alarm. The shrill alert had become dreadful for Jack over the last year, waking him every day to face a reality he had grown to hate. The only difference today was he was already wide awake by the time the alarm went off as the California sun peeked through the blinds. Today was the day that his prospective client was going to pull the trigger on the largest deal in Jack's company's history.

After scrolling through the morning news and checking his email, Jack finally got up and made his way to the adjoining bathroom to get ready. He stopped and looked at the man he saw in the mirror. He had been avoiding truly looking at himself for some time because he was afraid what he would see. Staring back at him was a beleaguered, tired, and spiritless man. Jack knew that he couldn't fake it anymore, but he had to just one more time today. Today was the big day—the one that could save everything—and he tried to muster as much good nervous energy he could while staring into his unrecognizable reflection.

"Let's go!" he told himself. "We win this deal and everything will change. It'll be back to the good times and I'll be my old self again. Make it happen like you used to, Jacky!"

Jack put on his lucky deal-closer shirt—a blue-and-gray-checkered oxford—and made his way downstairs. He walked into his dark and empty kitchen to brew his morning coffee. Jack used to love these types of mornings. The beautiful, misty California sunrise would be signaling a fresh start to another day of life. The kids would be clamoring over each other in the pantry picking out their favorite cereal with anticipation for a new day. His wife would be packing peanut butter and jelly sandwiches for all of them as Jack fired up the coffee and rang out positive energy to get the family started off right. His kids would roll their eyes at his daily affirmations of "Today is a great day for a great day!" and "Anything is possible if you just believe!" On big deal-closing days, he would involve the family in a semi-ritual to see how they should celebrate when work was over to put the positive energy out there that the deal would happen. But on this day, as Jack sat there alone and in his own thoughts, he couldn't help but think back to those amazing mornings and how symbolic this cold and empty kitchen was to his life right now.

Jack wanted to get to his office early so he could be in his own zone in case his prospective client called him before traditional working hours. He closed the door and walked to his car in silence—no goodbyes to his wife still sleeping or to the kids upstairs back from college break. As he put the car in reverse and started backing out of the driveway, his phone buzzed. Jack looked over, his stomach in knots, and saw it was just his VP texting him. "Today's the day, my man. Let's get another big one like the old times. See you in a few."

As he drove down the street, he glanced at his beautiful home in the rearview mirror and began to reflect on where he was in life. He had come so far and achieved so much in the eyes of society, but he was on the verge of losing everything that mattered to him. He couldn't help but wonder where all it went wrong.

This wasn't what life used to be for Jack. He had been in sales for twenty years now, and by all standards had an extremely successful career. He thought back to the days when he was a young gun cold-calling prospects from his little cubicle to quickly climbing the ranks to an Enterprise Account Executive working and closing million-dollar deals with Fortune 500 companies. He had had all the confidence in the world. His career brought not only great wealth from working with such large accounts but also high esteem throughout his organization for the man that could get deals done. Before he knew it, Jack had become addicted to the large commission checks and the company praise every time he was recognized for another monster deal.

Those commission checks also bought him his mansion in Laguna Beach, California, that was quickly fading in his rearview mirror. He and his family had taken exotic vacations all over the world. He had tremendous job security and flexibility. He was living what most called the American Dream. But that had all begun to change the last three years. As Jack's ego ballooned, his sales numbers declined. He started working longer hours to compensate. The career challenges also began to carry over into his personal life, where his constant negative attitude and the lack of presence at home began to erode his relationships with his wife and kids.

To make matters worse, he was living a lifestyle that depended on him having high sales results. The mortgage for his large house, the kids' college tuition, and all the social clubs he belonged to depended on a certain income that Jack had been accustomed to achieving. What was once a comfortable and lavish lifestyle was now incurring high interest rates and increasing credit card debt.

Jack turned his attention back to the road and tried to optimistically look forward versus backward. The one thing he was holding onto was this career-changing deal. He had won plenty of big deals in his two decades of B2B Enterprise Software Sales but nothing as big as this current opportunity with one of the largest Fortune 500 companies in the world. He had spent years cultivating the account, getting it in the buying cycle, and now had the potential to get pen to paper to officially land them as the marquee and largest customer for his organization. It would get him well past his annual quota, and likely earn him the coveted "Account Executive of the Year" award. The commission alone would pay off all his debt, and the momentum of such a big win would revitalize his career as he reclaimed the number one sales rep title in his company (an unofficial title that Jack wouldn't admit he held more important than his family).

As he pulled into his office, he made one glance at himself in the rearview mirror, noting how his eyes reflected the years of pressure he had carried over this massive deal. "Don't worry, Jack, it all changes today. Once they sign, all your problems will be over and then you'll be able to focus on bringing meaning back into your life."

Jack made his way into the office, trying to keep his steps as soft as possible and avoiding eye contact. He told himself he needed to be in the zone, but if he was honest, he would admit he didn't want to be seen. Soon enough he would be the hero again, but now he just wanted to keep to himself and get to his office as fast as possible.

Once he made it and closed the door, the waiting game began. Jack had always hated this part. He loved to be the man in control, and it was these final moments while waiting for a decision that he had none. Jack paced the room talking to himself for twenty minutes trying to remain calm and positive and ignore the knot weaving itself deep in his gut. "Once I pay off all the bills, then I can have enough to get Patti something really nice. I'll take the kids somewhere fun for vacation next summer. I know I haven't been the best husband or father lately, but I'll make up for lost time these last few years."

Then the phone rang.

At first fear struck, and Jack wondered if he should even answer it. He had been waiting for this moment all year, but deep down he did not have that great feeling of belief that he typically would have carried into the office on these types of deal-signing days. He made one last plea to the universe as he took a deep breath to muster up all his courage and looked up making his case to the world, saying, "Please, I need this!" before answering.

"Hey, Robert, so are we finally making this happen and becoming partners today?"

"I am so sorry, Jack, but the board met extensively the last week, and the project has to be postponed until next year. Given the uncertain economic conditions, we just can't commit the resources or the expansive budget needed to make a contractual decision this year. We really like what your company has to offer and want to re-visit down the line, but unfortunately now is not the time. My team wants to thank you for the enormous amount of time you have spent on us to this point. Enjoy the holidays with the family, and we'll be in touch next year."

"Thank you, Robert, I understand. Have a great holiday also."

Jack dropped his phone onto the desk, stunned at what had just happened. The realization and the enormity slowly began to sink in. All the hope Jack had held out to salvage an already challenging year was now officially gone. He was going to post his lowest quota attainment as a professional salesman in twenty years, which after his mediocre results the previous year, certainly meant the possibility of termination. There was no large commission check coming to pay off the increasing pile of debt or help save the financial strain that was sending his marriage to the brink of divorce. There would be no company adulation that Jack had so desperately worked for his entire career. The professional, personal, and financial stresses had finally taken its toll.

The blood rushed to his head, and he started to feel lightheaded. His knees weakened. With no more fight to give and all hope lost, Jack collapsed helplessly to the floor. He literally and figuratively hit rock bottom.

Jack began to feel as if he was floating above his body, and stared at his collapsed body on the floor of his office wondering, *Is this it? Is this what my life really came to? Agonizing over a deal that didn't happen? This isn't how it's supposed to end. I have so much more to accomplish. I need to repair my family and be there for my kids as they become adults. I still need time to accomplish my dreams and become the man I was supposed to be!*

As he floated there, reflecting on his life to this point, old hopes and dreams he had long since abandoned flashed before his eyes. You see, Jack's dream and career aspiration wasn't always to be a software salesman and make a lot of money. As a young boy, Jack, or Sonny as his friends called him, had one true love: golf. He was captivated by the game the first time he felt the clean stroke of a golf swing vibrate through his body. He felt it in synchrony with the pure sound of the club hitting the ball perfectly on the sweet spot, launching it into the sky. He loved losing himself in the game on a beautiful summer night, playing well into the darkness until he couldn't read the greens so that he could putt by feel.

His father worked two jobs to make ends meet. He was a full-time PE teacher at the local high school where he also helped out as a volunteer golf coach. During the summer and on the weekends, he would work as a starter at a nearby golf course and, due to the respect he had in the community, was given the privilege to allow his young son Sonny to practice on the range and play the course after all the late tee times had teed off. He took full advantage, and by the time he made it to the high school team to play for his dad, he was one of the better players in the region.

Jack was also a very popular student with plenty of friends. He had a huge personality, a warm heart, and an ability to connect with so many different types of people (probably a trait that led to his rapid success in sales). He valued relationships at an early age and always told himself that his family and friendships would come first no matter what. He had his identity and dreams all figured out. He was going to play golf in college, hopefully play professionally as long as it would allow, then move back home with all his friends and coach golf at the very high school his father did.

He made it to the golf part to play at San Diego State University, but a bad back led to multiple surgeries and the end of his competitive golf career. He began working at a golf course throughout college to stay close to the game and to ultimately pursue a career as a golf pro. When he was on the course, he felt alive in a way he never did anywhere else, even if it meant instructing rather than playing. But soon he was twenty-five years old and a married father of two. The long hours at the course and the low pay wasn't allowing him to be the provider his family needed him to be. Thus, Jack networked with some of the wealthy businessmen that played at the course to land an entry-level sales job where the ability to earn income was uncapped based on how much you sold.

Weekends off, a bigger paycheck, and more time with his family sounded very appealing to

Jack. He could even find time to play golf for himself now leisurely instead of just working at the golf club. At twenty-five, Jack's life plans and career dreams changed. He traded his golf clubs for a desk and a phone. For a little over a decade, Jack never looked back. But as his spirit looked down at his now forty-five-year-old unconscious body, he couldn't help but question the meaning of his life. If this was his final breath, had he truly lived the life he was supposed to live?

CHAPTER 2

The Diagnosis

"The good news is that we can work to treat this. The bad news is that if you don't make some serious life changes, the next time you might not wake up," the doctor stated to Jack at the hospital.

All the compounding stress of the last few years had taken its toll on Jack, and once he lost the one glimmer of hope he had, his body just shut down. Jack had experienced a severe heart attack. Thankfully for Jack, he had a guardian angel that morning. One of Jack's best friends and longtime teammate had an office adjacent to his.

His friend's wife, who happened to be a doctor, had to drop him off that day and was in the office grabbing a few of his things to take with her. When they heard the loud thud of Jack collapsing next door, she was able to provide immediate care for Jack after his collapse and save him in time for the paramedics to arrive.

"You are one lucky guy. If she hadn't been there to tend to you right away, you likely would have died. Timing is everything in this world, and just be thankful timing was on your side today."

"Yeah, I guess I had one thing going for me, though if I would have just closed my deal, this could have all been avoided," Jack mumbled under his breath.

Jack was diagnosed with high blood pressure and coronary artery disease and was instructed to take some time to relax and reprioritize his health. Another episode like the one he just had could certainly lead to death. His wife and kids were waiting for him in the waiting room.

"We love you, Daddy!" exclaimed Jack's little girl (though not so little anymore, as she was entering her sophomore year of college) Cassie.

"I don't know what I would have done without you, Dad," his son Will said gravely.

As Jack hugged both his kids, he was having trouble seeing the positives as reality began to sink back in. His career was likely in ruins, and he knew he would inevitably have to take out another loan to continue to pay for his children's college tuition. As he embraced his wife, he almost felt like he deserved this—karma for neglecting his family and punishment for not being able to be the provider he once was. Jack felt like a failure with no true meaning to his life.

When Jack first started in software sales, he had the perfect work-life balance. He firmly believed in the saying, "Work smarter, not harder." His autonomy allowed him to dictate his own schedule and go on many surprise adventures with his family. But eventually, the more successful he became, the more he craved even bigger deals. Over time, his long weekends with the family turned into extra hours logged at the office. Sporting events were missed, dinners routinely involved some type of screen, and gone were the spontaneous family vacations. Maybe most surprising, Jack even abandoned the game he loved so much and had gone years without swinging a club.

As Jack left the hospital facing his new reality, he received a phone call from his VP, Richard. "Jack, how are you doing, man? You gave all of us at the office a pretty good scare."

"Yeah, I guess all the pressure of these deals finally caught up to me. I just got diagnosed with coronary artery disease, and the doc instructed me to take it easy a while. I told him it's Q4 and we still have some big company targets to hit." Then Jack sighed. "I'm sorry I let you down, Richard. I know you were counting on me to bring that one home, and I'm ashamed of the results I'm going to put up this year."

Jack held his breath, waiting for the worst. Sales results were the bottom line in his profession. He and Richard had grown incredibly close over the years. But Richard demanded a lot from his employees and always put high pressure on his team to deliver the numbers they were expected to hit. Jack had no pipeline for the rest of the year, was going to have the worst sales results of his career, and his breakdown had been seen by everyone at the office. He felt like a failure in a business that doesn't provide much leeway to those who don't produce.

"Look, Jack, we all wanted this one, but this happens in our profession. Who knows, maybe they'll come back around next year. But I know it was a tough year for you professionally, so we're going to put you on paid sick leave for the next three weeks through the end of the year, at which point we'll determine what the best position is for you moving forward."

"I appreciate that offer, but this is the biggest time of the year for us. I can work to find something else to close for this year," begged Jack, but Richard wasn't budging.

"We both know you don't have anything else coming in, Jack, so please, take the time to enjoy with your family during the holidays and to get the help you need to get better. You've done a lot for this company over the years and have earned the right to take this time to prioritize getting yourself mentally and physically better. We'll sync after the final Q4 push to strategize and discuss next year. Glad you're still here, man. Some things are more important than work."

For Jack, it almost felt like a firing, and he didn't even process any of the positives Richard had said. In his mind, he was being placed on leave during the most important time of the year for his profession and Richard had been very noncommittal about his future. Jack was lucky to be alive and had just survived a massive heart attack, but even then, he barely could see the bright side that he was being blessed with a second chance at life. Like the last few years, work still totally consumed him, and now he was completely lost without it. With no idea where to turn or what to do next, Jack couldn't help but think maybe it would have been best for all if his large deal wasn't the only thing lost that day.

CHAPTER 3

The Mirror

"What an awful day. Let's get out of here," Jack grunted to his family.

This should have been a positive and thankful moment, but the negative energy that had surrounded Jack's family lately hung over them like a dark cloud.

"Let me drive, Jack," his wife Patti implored him.

"NO," Jack told her emphatically. "I'm fine, the only thing that isn't is the fact my pain-in-the-ass customer wasted a year of my life and time leading me to believe they were going to do something this year. It's a complete joke, and so is the doctor and his diagnoses. I am done with everything!"

"Well, glad to know we're such a priority in your life, Jack," Patti replied.

"I don't need to hear it, Patti. Give me the keys to my Range Rover. Only reason you have this car is because of my sales. And these aren't going to exist anymore if I keep having to deal with potential clients who screw me over!"

"Maybe you should stop blaming your clients or your family and look in the mirror, Jack." Patti tossed the keys at him and slammed the door as she climbed in the passenger seat.

Will and Cassie looked at each other in sadness as they slowly climbed into the back. This was not the dad they knew and loved. As kids and going into high school, their dad was their ultimate hero. He had such a great enthusiasm in their growth, provided incredible experiences most kids dreamed of, and gave them the feeling that anything was possible in life. Now, they were just scared that they may never see that type of father again.

After ten minutes of silence driving back from the hospital, Cassie, who got her outgoing personality from Jack, finally had to break the air.

"Dad, I don't know what happened with your sales deal, but you are still here. That has to count for something, right?"

Jack didn't answer as he stayed fixated on the road.

"Right! Say something, Dad."

Jack finally lost it. "You want me to say something, fine! Half of me wishes they would have left me there on the ground to die. This isn't the life I was supposed to live. I had big plans, big dreams! I should be finishing my career on the PGA Tour, or at the very least a big sales executive across a company and not having to deal with particular clients that can ruin your year. Now I am just a washed-up, middle-aged sales guy. What's the point of life? I have no purpose. I am a failure at my job. The world and this family are better off without me. What is even worth living for anymore? My life is done."

It was a heavy response for Patti, Will, and Cassie to internalize. On one hand, it was a big slap in the face that their husband and father found no purpose in the family they had. While at the same time, they all realized what a bad spot Jack was in and that he may need some serious help.

As the family pulled into their Laguna Beach hillside house, Patti grabbed Jack to the side before they entered the house.

"Look, Jack, I am not going to pretend to know the pressures you face as the financial provider for this family and someone your company leans on. But what I do know is that we need you. Not your bank account or the awards in your office—those mean nothing. I need a husband to help me raise two beautiful kids that are entering one of the most confusing, challenging, but rewarding times of their lives. This has been going on for two years now where we've just been getting by. And I'm not talking about financially. I won't live like this anymore. Figure out what is important to you, or I'll take Will and Cassie and leave this all behind. You say you are done with everything, well so am I. But at least I see the blessing we have in this family. Again, I suggest you go look at the man in the mirror and stop blaming everyone else."

Jack forcefully broke free of Patti and stormed upstairs without saying a word. "Man, what a day," he mumbled to himself as he fell into the chair in his bedroom. As he sat there in silence, the gravity and weight of the situation started to crush his soul. He was embarrassed that he couldn't deliver for the company like he used to. He was ashamed the way he had just acted in front of those he loved most. And most of all, he was sad that he had lost that passion for life that he was so known for since being a little kid.

Jack took a big breath as everything hit him at once, and he made his way to the bathroom. He slowly turned his attention to the giant mirrors to his right and stared at the man he had become. He saw a man that was exhausted with no zest for life, evident by the tired bags under his eyes. He saw a man with no confidence and no action, highlighted by his bloated and sullen face. But what really troubled him was that he saw a man with no soul behind those eyes. A man with no compassion, a man with no direction, and a man with no meaning. A man that couldn't even stand the face he saw in the mirror. Without warning, Jack cracked. The anger and rage he had been clinging onto burst out of him, and he unloaded of barrage of punches onto the mirror, until the only thing he could see was the blood from his hands spilling out on the sink below and the cracked reflection of a broken man.

CHAPTER 4

The Omen

"What was that, Jack?" screamed Patti as she rushed upstairs amid the commotion. She took one glance at the shattered mirror, then at Jack. "Are you serious? What have you done? Are you seriously going to act like this in front of our children? You almost died. Thankfully by the grace of God, a doctor was there to give you immediate care to keep you alive. Yet you can't find any blessings in what happened to still have a life to live. That is not the man I married. The man I knew would always find the positive things in life and make it work. I love you,

Jack, and I choose to believe that you were saved for a reason. But until you know that for yourself and start to prioritize what really matters in life, you are not welcome in this house. Put some bandages on and do whatever you need to do and go wherever you need to go. But I suggest you do some serious soul searching!"

Jack lowered himself to the bathroom floor and said nothing. He had hit rock bottom. After a few moments, he complied with Patti's wishes and patched himself up and went for a walk as he reflected on Patti's words. He had not given much thought to God or cultivated his spiritual life for a long time.

Jack grew up in a Catholic family, but through his teenage years, Sundays at church were replaced with rounds on the golf course. As Jack had grown into his older years, he viewed God in a more spiritual manner instead of a religious manner. He always had a strong spiritual faith about him that guided his life, but the more he became consumed with his work and lifestyle, the less he tapped into that spiritual energy with God. With no work to pursue and now walking alone with his thoughts, Jack began talking to God about what had been burning in his soul.

"God, I know I haven't made you much of a priority, but I don't know who else to turn to. What is the meaning of life? If no one had been there to save me today, would I have fulfilled my destiny and become the man I was meant to be? I thought I was walking my path when things were going great all those years, but now I have no idea if I'm living a good life. I'm forty-five years old with a disease that can potentially end it all, my career is likely over, my kids are on their way to be on their own, and my wife can hardly look at me. I thought I was successful with the career achievements and all the money I made, but well, I just don't know anymore. What exactly did all of that get me? If I died right now on this walk, how do I know if I truly lived out my purpose and had a successful life?"

They were powerful questions that on the surface Jack had been avoiding addressing. He was comfortable in the image, career, and life he had created. But asking these types of questions about purpose and meaning were leading to answers for years he hadn't wanted to hear. Deep down he had been asking them for a long time, even when on the outside he appeared to be living the American Dream. After the initial thrill of a big sale or commission check ran out, he always wondered if there was more to life. When the questions arose, he would put them off and continue on with his normal routine. But now with no routine, no vision, and on the brink of losing it all, he was ready to start asking.

Jack continued on his walk and instantly felt a little better in the quiet of the nature as he finally confronted his internal voice. Jack typically walked like he lived: fast and on a mission to get to the next task. But today, he slowed it down. He was a long way from wanting to face his family after his breakdown in the bathroom, and for once, he was finding a small glimmer of peace of just *being* and not worrying.

Something in his gut told him to take the long route through the park connected to his neighborhood, so Jack finally listened. *What else do I have to do on this beautiful day in Southern California?* he thought. He made his way through the park, and a white object grabbed his attention out of the corner of his eye. Jack walked over and bent down to find a perfectly clean golf ball in the grass. He picked it up to closely examine it. It had been a while since he had last touched a golf ball, and Jack felt an energy course through his body he hadn't felt in a long, long time. As he examined it, he envisioned the ball flying into the blue sky, closely felt the hundreds of dimples that gave it character, and identified a small number two printed under the brand logo.

One of the powerful forces in Jack's early success was that he was always cognitive of the tiny omens that God seemed to put in his life when he tapped into that spiritual connection. Sometimes it was a large omen that heavily impacted a decision, or sometimes it might have been a small coincidence that Jack knew very well was more than some random occurrence. Back then, he believed strongly in the forces of the universe that the higher power God used to help guide people.

Jack's father taught him at a very early age about these signs God would put in his life, directing him toward his path. When something happened that was almost too crazy to believe it was coincidence, he told Jack to take that as a sign from the universe that he was walking the correct path. "As long as you continue to look for them, they will always be there," he would tell young Jack.

Well, older Jack had stopped looking, and the signs had stopped showing. That was until now, in that moment when Jack held that golf ball in his hand. Jack had always been drawn to the number two. His birthday was on February 2, and he was supposed to have a twin brother who had unfortunately died midway through the pregnancy. Anything that had to do with the number two was always an omen in Jack's eyes that his brother's spirit was guiding him from above.

Now that number appeared on a random golf ball in an empty park. Golf was the foundation of his relationship with his now late father, and thinking of that, the ball gave him a slight glimmer of hope. Golf was always more than a game to him. It had given him joy and anticipation for most of his early life. It was a sport that had helped shape the young and successful man he once was. This was no coincidence. His gut feeling had told him to take this path, and now he suddenly understood why. He still didn't know the answers to the questions burning inside of him about the meaning of life. And if he had died, he wasn't sure whether his life would have been a success. But at least now, holding that golf ball, he knew what to do next.

Chapter 5

The Caddie

"Wow, I forgot what it was like to see the sunrise," Jack said to himself as he was making his way south down the California coast. The sun was peeking over the mountains to the east with an array of purple and dark orange lighting up the early-morning sky. Just off the highway to the west, the Pacific waves glistened with a golden glow to them as they made their way to the shoreline. The combination of both sights would humble any man with its beauty.

In the past, when he would drive down south to San Diego for business appointments, he was always in such a rush that he routinely failed to take in the beauty that surrounded him during his drive. But today there was no business to attend to. Instead, Jack was going to play golf. When he found the golf ball in the park, he knew he needed to go back to the beginning to find what he was looking for. Golf had always provided him with a sense of purpose and had funny ways to teach him life lessons through the years. Perhaps getting back on the course would help Jack get some direction back to his life.

As Jack pulled into the golf course, a sense of calm came over him. He knew embarking on this retreat by himself was the right decision. He had scheduled an early tee time that day, hoping to be the first person off to have the round to himself. When he had stopped playing golf competitively, it had become much more of a social outing for him. He would take clients out for a round early Friday or use it as an excuse so he could get out on the course and have some beer with his buddies. But when he first fell in love with the game as a kid, it was the individuality aspect of the game that really drove him to it. It was just him, the ball, and the beautiful nature of that moment. He would lose himself in the moment and learn more about himself than in any other thing he did.

Since it had been quite some time that he last played, Jack stopped at the driving range to get some practice in before he teed off. He could tell he was rusty, but after a few swings, that amazing feeling of perfect contact began to coarse through his blood. As Jack was finishing up his bucket of balls, he noticed an old man slowly approaching him. "Nice swing you got there. Looks like you won't need too many pointers today, though not even the greats never stop learning," said the old man smiling. "Nice to meet you. Everyone around here just calls me Caddie. I'm going to be joining you on your round today!"

"The name is Jack. I didn't know that caddies were required for this course."

"Well, have you played here before?"

"Long time ago. I remember it being one of my favorites back when I played down here regularly."

"Lot has changed since then. Don't worry. I won't bother too much. Maybe just a few tips here and there. A little advice couldn't hurt, right? Plus, I get to carry your bag," joked the caddie to make light of the situation.

Jack had been hoping to have this time to himself for personal reflection. He loved those lone summer nights when it was just him on the course. That was what he wanted to recreate in his search for enlightenment. But he had driven over an hour to play this course, and he was the only one in his tee time, so he begrudgingly agreed to have the caddie assist.

"Well, if you say so, sir. Tee time is in fifteen minutes, if you wouldn't mind cleaning my clubs before the round, I am going to practice my short game."

"You got it, boss," the caddie happily exclaimed back to Jack.

He seems awful cheery for a chilly Wednesday morning at the crack of dawn, thought Jack as he walked to the practice putting green. He almost started questioning if this was the right idea as the negative voice Jack had become accustomed to hearing began to invade Jack's head.

As the caddie stood at the clubhouse washing Jack's clubs, he kept an eye on him down on the practice putting green. The caddie had come across many a fellow in his years working on the golf course. Golf has a funny way of showing the character of a man, and the caddie had a keen eye on sensing the type of man he was about to walk with based on how he carried himself on the course. As he examined Jack, the caddie knew he had seen this type of person before. A man who on the outside was lifeless with no energy, but inside him there was something great burning inside to come out.

CHAPTER 6

The First Tee

"What brings you on a morning before the holidays?" asked the caddie as he and Jack walked to the first hole to start the round.

Reluctant to respond, Jack gave a half-hearted answer, "Well, I had a few things come up at work that caused my company to give me time off through the holidays, so I figured I would dust off the old sticks and hit the links."

"Interesting. Well, I know a lot of folks who would give anything to have the flexibility to have the holiday season off this time a year, let alone play some golf during the week."

Jack, not wanting to engage in the conversation, brushed off the comment and continued walking. His energy had completely changed in the last few minutes. He was optimistic and excited to play golf after a few good practice swings, but as the round was set to start, he was clearly becoming agitated. Deep down, Jack had a hard time accepting that he was playing golf on a Wednesday during the biggest sales week of the year. The caddie knew he had his work cut out for him based on this powerful negative energy in Jack's orbit but was excited about the possibilities of connecting with a new soul during another unique round. He knew he would have to start from the beginning.

"It is beautiful, isn't it?"

"What is so beautiful?" questioned Jack annoyingly.

"Well, if you must ask, all of it. The sun rising above the mountains to the east. The trees swaying in the cool breeze along the perfectly cut fairway. The fact that here you are on another day on this earth playing a game as great as golf!

I am just thankful I get to experience something like this to start my day!"

"Yes, it is a nice course. But the ball isn't going to hit itself. Where should I aim off the tee to have the best angle into the green for my second shot?"

"Jack, can I ask you a simple question?"

"Sure, if you answer my question with a simple answer after that!"

"Fair enough. . . . Why are you here?" the caddie posed to Jack.

"Well, I suppose to kill my free time to play some golf."

"Just kill some free time, huh? Are you sure there is nothing in addition to that?"

"Nice question and good try. But I'm just an old golfer trying to get back into the game. Now can you please tell me where I should aim?"

"The game?" the caddie recited back to Jack. "Interesting concept, a game that is. Are we talking about the game of golf or the game of life?"

The question back hit him hard. Jack was trying to fight all this self-doubt and find meaning in his life, and here was this caddie he had known ten minutes challenging him about the game of life. For the first time since he had pulled into the parking lot, Jack let his guard down and became intrigued.

After a few moments of silence and recognizing the energy shift a bit, the caddie continued. "Jack, this amazing game of golf means more than just hitting a white ball in a hole as few times as possible. If you've played this sport significantly in the past, and by your tone and golf swing I am assuming you have, then I believe you already know this. Well, if this game means something to you, so can this round. We were put in each other's path for a reason today, and I firmly believe that. Now this round can go two ways. I can sit back and tell you where and how to put the golf ball on each hole to help you hit that ball as few times as possible. Or you can join me on a round of a lifetime, and I can teach you about the meaning and principles of golf and how you can translate these principles and mindsets toward the game of life. The beauty is, it is up to you. After all,

I am just a caddie," he said with a big smile on his face.

Meaning, reasoning, principles. These were all things Jack had been contemplating when he began evaluating his life since his health incident. He thought back to the ball he had found in the park a few days earlier. It had taken him some time to put it all together, but that omen had led him to this golf course, which in turn had led him to this caddie who was speaking about the very things that had been on Jack's mind. *This wasn't coincidence*, thought Jack; he was meant to be here. Maybe he wasn't supposed to find his way on his own like he had anticipated . . . maybe he was supposed to meet someone to guide him.

Jack had been yearning to get this off his chest, and he figured he barely knew this caddie anyway, so he finally let it out. "It's funny you used words like *meaning* and *principles*. You asked me why I was here. Well, truth be told, this game of life you speak of hasn't been the greatest to me as of late. I lost a major deal that my career was basically hanging on, I have driven my family to not want to be around me, and I don't even recognize the man I see in the mirror. I actually almost died recently. If I would have died, what would my legacy have been? How would I have known I lived a successful life and had become the man I was ultimately meant to be? With all my struggles recently, I guess I'm having a hard time answering these questions, and the one thing that has ever brought me clarity when I was younger was golf, so is that a better answer as to why?"

The Caddie continued, "First off, I appreciate you opening up about some of your problems. I could sense something heavy weighing on you, and I can already feel some of your burden being lifted! That is absolutely a better answer as to why. So let's do this! Just you, the ball, the course, and a few wise lessons an old man like me has learned throughout the years. Just like golf, I've experienced the highs and lows of life as well.

"You see, I was in a similar situation as you just after my sixtieth birthday. I questioned why I was here, who I was. Ultimately, my searching for the answers to those questions lead me to create the five foundational principles and five mindset mantras that I try to live by daily. As I began to incorporate these principles and mindsets into my daily actions and thoughts, I found myself living a happier and more meaningful life, and answering a lot of the questions you just asked. The beautiful thing is, these foundational principles and mindset mantras tend to show themselves on the golf course. That's how I discovered them. Over the years, I developed them to take with me on and off the course. I guess that should be no surprise coming from a caddie who has spent decades experiencing fairways and bunkers both in golf and in life. Maybe after eighteen holes, not only will you have a great round, but perhaps you will find some of the answers you are looking for as well!"

Jack cracked a quick and innocent smile, the first time he had smiled like that in a long time.

"I'll take that smile as an agreement." The caddie smiled back. "But I am curious. You said the game of life hasn't been that great to you as of late, and that you almost died. But here you are, still playing the most precious game of all!"

Jack started to feel ashamed that he had not shared the same perspective. He was so focused on this deal, his career, and his financial status that after almost losing the gift of life, Jack had yet to appreciate how fortunate he really was.

Sensing the reality sinking in, the caddie continued, "You have been given a great gift, Jack, the gift of realizing how precious life is. You could have died that day, but here you are able to truly understand that life can be taken from us at any moment, and you live to tell about it. Not everyone is offered that miracle."

"You're right. My coworker's spouse is a doctor and was in our office when I collapsed. She was able to give me immediate care that likely saved my life. I guess I was so focused on losing that deal and possibly my job that I didn't even see the angel that was there to save me. How could I have missed such an incredible blessing?" questioned Jack.

"It is easier than you think, Jack. People are wired to think about their problems instead of their blessings. But the man who lives a meaningful life centers his very core on a fundamental and foundational principle: **gratitude**.

Principle 1: Gratitude 

"Jack, I'm sure you've heard the saying 'Practice an attitude of gratitude.' And it may sound cliché, but this is the foundational principle of all five of the principles I mentioned. Every day we wake up is a blessing that we should be thankful for! By practicing gratitude daily and being thankful for both our blessings and our problems, we begin to recognize the beauty of life and begin to live with more meaning. Just today you chose to focus your negative energy on the disappointment that you weren't in the office, rather than recognizing the blessing of having time to yourself to play a game that you love. But we can always find meaning in our challenges and problems if we look at them through a lens of gratitude, just as we can be incredibly thankful when a great blessing and reward touches our life. As a wise man once told me, 'Expect nothing but appreciate everything!' If you want to transform your life and live a life of meaning and happiness, embrace the principle of gratitude and control your attitude to act on it! We can't control our circumstances, but we can control how we respond to them!"

Jack quickly realized that he was a man that was not centered around gratitude. When sales weren't going his way to live this larger-than-life persona he built, he didn't look at it through a form of gratefulness that he had a job that allowed him to sell and provide the necessities in life. Maybe this was a sign from the universe that there was more to life than his commission check and that he needed to realize this. When his wife would beg him to spend quality time with her, he looked at it with annoyance rather than seeing how there are many people who yearn to have a significant other that loves them so much and just wants them to be present. When he almost died, he felt like a complete failure and didn't recognize the great blessing that someone was in the office that day that could provide immediate help to Jack and ultimately a second chance at life.

Finally, Jack spoke. "I guess I've never really looked at it like that. When things were going well, I made it appear that it was me who was so great. When things would go wrong, it certainly wasn't my fault, so I blamed the circumstances. But I can see now that, at the end of the day, I am going to experience both rewarding successes and mighty challenges, but if I can cultivate that attitude of gratitude, it becomes less about myself and more about appreciating *life* itself."

"Exactly, Jack! It is important to note though if you can appreciate all the good things in your life and see it as a blessing over a personal achievement, you inevitably take a form of gratitude. The hard part is finding the blessing when you experience those challenges, failures, and losses. That is when true gratitude practice takes place and ultimately when real happiness and meaning fill your soul. The great thing is, it is a choice, Jack! You decide how you are going to respond to everything in life, and perhaps that is the biggest blessing of all!"

"We've yet to hit my tee shot, and I feel like I've learned more about life and perspective in the last five minutes than I have the last five years," laughed Jack.

"Well, we're just getting started. There are many principles to guide your life, and we will touch on more, but at the very core of any foundation you need to build something sturdy that will stay strong against the test of time. There is nothing sturdier than living every day with an attitude of gratitude! But as promised, back to your original question. You see that tree about two hundred fifty yards away on the right of the fairway? Aim just to the left of that, and there is a slope that if hit correctly will roll the ball toward the middle of the fairway another fifty yards."

Jack closed his eyes and finally started to look up and within. "Thank you, God. Thank you for letting me still be here. Thank you for providing me with a great life and with a wonderful family around me. Thank you for putting that little golf ball in my path when I was lost and finding this caddie to help give me a much-needed perspective on life. Thank you for this opportunity to play a game I love so much."

The caddie stood there in silence as he knew Jack was beginning to look at today from a lens of gratitude, and the caddie was just as thankful God had placed Jack in his path as well.

Jack opened his eyes, grabbed his driver, and let it rip! He hadn't hit a ball that far in a long time, as all the positive energy Jack suddenly had pulsing through his body created more power than he knew possible. Jack looked at the caddie and winked as he executed his first drive to perfection. The extra fifty yards of roll once the ball landed didn't hurt either.

CHAPTER 7

The Stroll on the Second

"Okay, I'll give credit where credit is due—nice advice, Caddie! Always good to start the round with a par. Thanks for the tip on where to hit it. And even more than that, thanks for teaching me the foundation of gratitude. I'm going to start to practice incorporating it in my life." Jack high-fived the caddie with appreciation.

"Finding gratitude in the moment puts your mind at ease, doesn't it?" replied the caddie. "It's incredible the great things you can accomplish when you're able to relax and find gratitude in the moment."

Jack and the caddie made their way over to the second hole, a long dogleg left Par 5 that had water to the left and a line of trees to the right. It was a challenging hole, but one of the more beautiful on the course. A par on the first had lit life back into Jack. It was his first time playing golf in years, and he had played that hole perfectly. With this newfound energy, his mind already began to imagine the possibilities of a low-scoring round. As he got up to the tee, he pulled out his driver and cut it perfectly along the edge of the pond to set up his second shot. Jack walked quickly with excitement to his ball to get ready.

"Let's go, Caddie. Looks like it didn't take long to get the swing back."

The caddie smiled and nodded his head. Feeling like his old confident self, Jack didn't take long to get to his ball and let his swing go again. Another perfect hit ball to the middle of the fairway set him up for a great approach with an easy wedge a hundred yards into the green. Jack was walking so quickly with excitement that he soon found himself twenty yards ahead of the caddie.

"Keep up, you old man. With another perfect shot here, we can get on the birdie train!"

But the caddie strolled at the same leisurely pace he usually did. As he finally got up to the ball with Jack eagerly waiting, he posed a simple question, "Why the hurry, Jack?"

"I am feeling it, man! Gotta keep the momentum going!"

"Keep it going to what, Jack?"

"To hopefully a birdie and negative numbers! Am I missing something here?"

"Funny you ask again! As you were running up to your ball with eagerness to hit your next shot, there was no way you could have seen the radiating reflection of the morning sun on the pond. Or feel the gentle breeze of the Pacific that carries with it hints of salt in the air. Or hear the birds chirping in symphony that they get to create music on another beautiful morning day. The perfect symmetry of all the senses coming together to create this one magical moment that will never look, feel, smell, or hear the same way again. So yes, I would say you actually missed a lot."

"Well that all sounds blissful, but I am not out here to take pictures or get lost in nature, I am out here to score the lowest round possible."

"Jack, I think this is a great time to introduce and explain foundational principle two here on the second hole. Society today has created this standard that we need to rush from one accomplishment or task to another. I haven't known you long, but in your profession, I would compare it to wanting to get to the close of a sale for that instant gratification and then begin working immediately on the next one. Now I am not discounting wanting to get that sale as quickly as you can—that is your job. But you should not be entirely focused on the end result. There is beauty in that entire sales process. From the relationships and connections you build within the account, to the challenges you help them solve, to finally all coming together in unity to one commercial agreement. You should be present and enjoy the entire process. That is the essence of foundational principle two: **presence.** Being present, enjoying the process, and living in the moment!

Principle 2: Presence 

Jack started thinking. He knew this type of thinking intimately. When he would get a lead or introduced to the account, the first thing he thought about was the end result and the commission possible of the sale that would benefit him. But what Jack hadn't considered was that the sales process is a journey with another business and other humans, and he should embrace every interaction that leads to the end result.

"You're right, Caddie, I've been guilty of this for most of my life. Our culture rewards achieving as many successes as you can, and I guess that carries over to my career and how I also look at the game of golf going from one shot to the next. How did you know?"

"Let's call it a hunch. Look at a round of golf; a great golf round encompasses more than just the shots and results of the score. If you are only focused on the end result and getting to the next shot, you are missing beautiful things along the entire journey. One of the beautiful things about golf is the amazing scenery and purposeful architecture of the course. We only recognize that beauty when we truly are living in the moment. You can live in the moment by enjoying the walk between shots and tuning in to all your senses. As it is in life, the journey of the round is far more meaningful than the end result itself. And we find that meaning by incorporating presence in our life in all that we do!

Jack began to feel a sense of guilt by thinking of all the moments he missed by not being present. From working at home and worrying about his job rather being in the moment with his wife and kids, to the hundreds of times he failed to take in the inspiring beauty of Southern California during his commute between customers while solely focusing on the duty at hand. Almost on cue, the caddie continued with his lesson.

"It is not an easy habit to master, Jack. A great illustration of this actually came in the Disney movie *Soul*. A man, similar in age to yourself, worked his entire life to be a mainstage musician, a dream that had consumed his life. And when his opportunity had finally arrived, he took a misstep in the city streets and fell to this death.

All he could think about was being robbed of that opportunity and getting back to life to achieve that goal. Through the movie, he actually earns the right to go back to the world and the souls of the universe asked him what he was going to do. While thinking, he flashed back to all the little moments he took for granted. Like standing with his feet in the waves of the ocean or the taste of a great pizza. He proudly proclaimed he was just going to *live*! So take heed from that story, Jack, that whatever it is that you are doing in that moment, do it with *presence*. If you are at home with your family, *be with them*. If you are on the golf course, *be here every step you take*. Enjoy every moment, Jack, because as you now know, life can be taken from you without any warning."

Jack nodded in acknowledgment. He thought back to the moment he floated above his own body, wondering whether he had lived a meaningful life. He realized that it wasn't just meaning that was missing. He was constantly living in the future. To the next sale, to the next commission check, to the next big achievement. Even in that dream, he remembered thinking there was so much to accomplish. To live a meaningful life, Jack had to quit reminiscing on past successes, stop worrying about what the future would bring, and start *living in the present!*

The caddie immediately sensed that this principle had hit Jack right in the heart. Jack didn't respond with words or excuses; he just took a deep breath and approached his ball. Jack's only focus was keeping his head down and swinging his body in perfect harmony as he had done a thousand times before. The caddie watched as Jack executed with extreme focus on the details of his swing as the club struck the ball perfectly, shooting up high in the air toward the flag. The ball landed softly and checked up just below the slope within seven feet to the hole for an uphill birdie putt. Unlike the last two shots, Jack didn't rush up to admire the absolute beauty of the wedge shot he had just hit. That moment was over. It was only a hundred-yard walk up to the green, and Jack was going to enjoy every step. He looked around at the intricacies of the hole in awe of its precise layout with the mountains in the background providing a natural stadium setting for this hole alone. He knew he would remember the beauty of the hole and this moment for the rest of his life, while also acknowledging the three perfect shots along the way.

CHAPTER 8

The Blow-Up

After such a memorable hole and a one-putt birdie, Jack and the caddie made their way to the third hole. For not having played in some time, starting par-birdie on the first two holes was as good a scenario as Jack could think of. After his previous perspective on the moment, Jack was trying to slow himself down, but he was definitely amped up as he stood on the tee at three. It was a short Par 4, with a narrow fairway and hazards to both sides. The smart play would be to hit a wood or long iron and avoid going into the water on left or canyon area on the right. But if he hit a driver just right, he could potentially be on or near the green.

"Now, Jack, an easy four iron leaves you a nice pitching wedge in. Just hit it nice and straight out there and give yourself a good angle at the green."

"I respect your opinion, sir, but have you not seen those last two holes. I've never been one to play it easy. This is a hole you can take advantage on. Now give me the big stick!"

The caddie sort of smirked. "If you say so, boss."

As Jack addressed the ball and got into his stance, he knew that with his older age he would certainly have to get some power into this one to have any chance on getting it near the green. He gripped the club tight and roared it back faster than usual. He was trying so hard to get power on the ball that his whole body was in motion. His head was lifted high, his right elbow out loose, and his lower body was completely out of sync. As he started his down swing, his body was so in front of it with his arms out wide that he was unable to get into his usual finish position. As soon as he made contact, Jack knew and could only look up in angst as the ball kept slicing hard into the right into the oblivion of the canyon.

"Well, we aren't finding that one, Jack, are we?"

"Nope, guess not," a dejected Jack stated with his hand rubbing his temples.

Jack always wanted to avoid the blow-up hole and going OB off the tee was never the best start. Fortunately for the short distance, the dropped shot off the tee only cost Jack a bogey as he was able to get on close after his re-tee, in which he hit iron, and made a one-putt save. They made their way to the Par 3 fourth. This time, it was a long iron Par 3 with a small upward green that required perfect precision to give yourself a chance at two putting for par.

"Judging by your last few swings, Jack, when you hit it well you have a natural draw on your swing. If you get out of sync, you tend to miss right. If you can just focus on finishing with your normal swing and give it a nice draw, it should land perfectly on the downslope at the front right of the green and feed down into the pin."

"Got it, boss."

The bad slice from the last hole was still in Jack's mind. He knew another slice would leave his chances at par virtually impossible. So as most golfers do upon addressing the ball after a bad shot, Jack was repeating to himself in his head, "Make sure to stay down and stay compact—don't slice the ball!"

As he went to make his swing, he said it one more time. But all the mental thinking of not slicing caused Jack to put too much weight on his front leg as he shifted his hips to hit the draw, and instead he hooked the ball way left to the green.

"Dang it, man! One hole I slice into the woods, the next I'm hooking. You're better than this, Jack! Get it together!" he yelled to himself as he forcefully threw his club back in the bag without making eye contact at the caddie.

Fortunately, Jack was able to find his ball and had a good lie in the rough. But he left his pitch to about fifteen feet and could only muster a two putt to card back-back bogeys.

"From minus one to plus one just like that," mumbled Jack.

The duo made their way to the fifth hole, a long Par 5 that again would make him pay for any mishit off the tee. As Jack stood there examining the tough hole in front of him, he realized any chance to take advantage of the Par 5 required an excellent tee shot. He needed some advice, so he turned to the caddie who had suddenly turned quiet the last two holes as Jack struggled. But as soon as he turned to make one of his famous smart-ass remarks, the caddie began to speak.

"I was observing those last two tee shots of yours, Jack, and the good news is that it is a pretty simple fix. Any idea what it is?"

"Well, they both felt awkward, but you were watching; you tell me!"

"Yes, it probably did feel awkward because you were trying to do too much. Two holes ago you were trying to swing so hard with as much power as you could generate that you were almost completely out of your stance. By swinging so hard, you actually cost yourself the opportunity on that respective hole. The last hole, you were focusing and overcompensating so much not to slice again that it caused you to get way too in front of the ball resulting in that hook. I think now is the perfect time to talk about foundational principle three: **balance**."

Principle 3: Balance 

"In golf, you need to keep that foundation of balance throughout your entire shot if you want to make clean contact. By trying to use too much power or touch to stay in front, you're actually doing yourself more harm than good. The same principle is true in life. Let's look at some common scenarios our world faces daily where the principle of balance is abused. Work is an easy one. Some people get so consumed by their job that it takes over their life. They work so hard to be successful or advance up the corporate ladder that it is all they focus on. They may experience some short-term success but have a maniacal approach to live in a way that will ultimately do more harm than good. You will ultimately sacrifice your family or friends for your work, which in a lot of cases can ruin relationships. You can also burn yourself out quickly, resulting in severe emotional and physical stress. Now I'm not saying to not work hard. To become great at anything in life, you must have a strong work ethic. But you need to balance any endeavor worth working at with your other priorities in life, such as your health and relationships."

Jack understood. Five years ago, he had balance in his life, and he remembered it being some of his happiest times. But over the last five years, he had been totally consumed with his sales profession as the demands and stress of maintaining his lifestyle and delivering for the company mounted. As the caddie had just noted, the long-term effect of not balancing his job was now showing itself in the constant pressure of his career, his physical and mental health, and in the deteriorating relationships with his wife and kids. If there was one principle Jack may have been missing most in his life and that was causing these health, family, and financial issues, it was balance. The caddie continued with his lesson.

"I mean, our Creator found ways to instill this foundation as a principle we must master in our lives. Take a look at alcohol. A glass of wine with a nice dinner or a couple of beers with your friends after a round is an enjoyable and fun experience. But if you abuse the amount of alcohol you put into your body, you can become overly intoxicated and lose the capacity to make wise decisions while also waking up sick and hungover, to make matters worse. It's not bad to enjoy a warm cookie or a bowl of ice cream on a hot summer day. Guess what though, if you eat those every day, you aren't going to have a healthy body. The same can be said for physical exercise. To live a healthy life, exercise needs to be incorporated into your everyday life. But too much physical exercise can actually cause harm and pain to the body. Again, you need to find that balance. Can you see how everything you do, whether it be golf, work, wellness, and even your social habits, must apply some semblance of balance to live your most meaningful life?"

"One hundred percent, Caddie! Balance has been missing from my life for quite some time. I guess I never really thought how my decisions in the short-term to prioritize work over my family and relationships would have this type of long-term effect. I guess my whole life, when something was in front of me that I wanted to achieve, I would just go after it with all I had with no regard to how it was impacting myself or others," said Jack.

"Well, you aren't alone, Jack. Our culture rewards the story of the last man in the office. It idolizes celebrities who live these great social lives partying all day and night, or social influencers who have bodies with no fat on them. It causes people to go to great lengths to work longer, party harder, and workout stronger. Again, it is important to work hard to achieve success in your career, have social moments with friends, and incorporate exercise into your life. But if you begin overemphasizing any of these things and don't incorporate balance into the daily foundation of your life, you will ultimately do more harm than good. Just like your last two shots." The caddie smiled.

Jack began thinking of how little balance he had in his life. He had been working long hours, then partying into the night and paying hell for it the next day. He couldn't remember the last time he exercised—due to how much he was working—and would ultimately drink to relieve himself from the stress of working. He saw how by just applying this very principle a lot of the problems he now faced could have likely avoided. But then he also remembered to stay in the moment. That he couldn't change the past, only that he could live in the present and use his past to make wiser decisions for the future. His moment was now this golf swing, and he turned his attention to the ball.

The caddie could see Jack changing before his eyes. He knew Jack was reflecting on the very little balance he had in his life. And he also knew he was using the principle of living in the present to turn his attention back to that moment. When one starts using all the principles together, that is when real transformation happens, and one achieves self-realization.

"Remember, just stay balanced, Jack, and let the club do the work."

As Jack addressed the ball, he didn't worry about where he hit it or how hard. He just told himself to remain balanced, and if he did that, he would have a much greater outcome than his last two tee shots. Sure enough, Jack was able to find his rhythm and hit his driver square on the ball this time, sending the ball straight down the fairway and as long as he had ever hit it.

"Great shot, Jack! When you just focus on incorporating balance, you never do more harm than good. And ultimately that good usually becomes great! Amazing, right?!"

Jack high-fived the caddie. He knew that he had a lot of work to do to begin implementing the foundational principle of balance into his life. But he had just hit one of the best drives of his life, and he was going to enjoy the long walk to his ball and his next shot. He was learning!

CHAPTER 9

The Dots Always Connect

By the time he approached the Par 7, a tight Par 4 with trees along both sides, Jack had gotten his game back on track. He had birdied the hole after his monster drive and followed that up with a steady par to remain even at the moment. He knew the challenge ahead as he stared at the narrow fairway trying to decide if he should hit his driver again or play it smart with a long iron.

"What do you think here, Caddie, aggressive or play it smart?"

"Well, you did just have one of the best drives of your life two holes ago with your driver. This hole certainly rewards a great drive, as it opens up toward the green and leaves an easy pitch if you hit it straight. But at the same time, if you hit just a bit to the left or right you leave yourself in some serious trouble. You could go either way, Jack. Ultimately the decision is up to you. I would just go with your gut. "

Jack thought long and hard on the pros and cons of each. He wavered back and forth as he looked at each club. Finally, something told him deep down to hit the iron. He didn't know why, but he decided to go with it as he reached into the bag and grabbed his long iron. The caddie was intrigued to see how this would play out.

Jack went into his pre-shot routine with confidence that this was the club to hit. But as he swung the club, he let his shot get a little too loose, and the ball went to the right and disappeared into the woods. Any other hole he probably would have been fine. But this hole required perfect precision, and now Jack and the caddie were off to find his ball.

"Dang it! I just missed it! I knew I had the right club, how in the heck did that not hit the fairway? What a joke, I can't believe that. This game is the most unforgiving game of all time; sometimes I ask myself why I even try to play!"

The caddie just sat back and let Jack air out his frustration as they made their way into the trees on the search. It was a dense set of trees, and the sunlight barely made its way through to the bottom. They searched for about three minutes to no avail. The caddie was about to keep to the course rules and inform Jack he would have to declare a lost ball when a bit of sunshine fought through the trees and glinted its reflection off the tiny white ball.

"There, Jack, go see if that is yours!"

Jack made his way to the area the caddie pointed, and sure enough there was a ball. As Jack bent over, he saw his brand logo with the number two on the ball and was instantly relieved.

"Got it! Man, that is a nasty lie. Not sure how we are going to do this one."

The duo examined the ball and its position. It wasn't completely plugged, but it had been covered in mud as it traveled through the trees and dewy ground. But even more unforgiving was where it actually sat. There seemed to be no window to get this ball out to the fairway, let alone to the hole. As Jack stood over it, he saw a tiny gap in all the trees toward the hole.

"I think I got it, Caddie. Do you see what I'm seeing?"

"I don't see much, Jack. But if you see it, go for it. Remember, sometimes these are the fun shots in golf. If it was easy and we were playing from the middle of the fairway, everyone would do it!" the caddie said as he tried to make light of the tough situation.

"Yup, I got it! Give me the seven!"

Jack was lasered focused on that tiny gap. He would have to not only hit the muddy ball perfectly to get it launched in the air correctly, but also have to precisely hit his target between the trees. This was as tough a shot Jack had ever seen, but he was going to go for it. He lined up his seven, and as he addressed the ball, he mumbled to himself, "Let the club do the work, don't try too hard. Make a good swing and whatever happens, happens!"

As Jack swung his club down, fighting through all the debris and branches, he magically made clean contact and sent the ball soaring toward the sliver of green pastures behind it. The caddie stood behind tracking it and couldn't believe what he was seeing. The ball kept traveling and cleared through the woods unscathed, with no noise or ricochet off the trees.

"Be good, ball, be good!" exclaimed Jack. "That made it through, right? I can't believe it. I wonder where it is!" Jack's tone had changed drastically since he was cursing the game a few minutes back.

"I think we are good, Jack! Wow, what a shot. Let's go see where we are!"

They began walking toward the fairway to see if they could spot the ball. Due to the nature of the shot, they had no idea where it would have landed. As they scanned the fairway short of the green, they saw nothing. So they turned their attention toward the green, and they both stopped right in their tracks. The ball was within two feet of the cup for an easy tap-in birdie!

"Would you look at that, Caddie! I take back everything I said after the poor tee shot."

"That is truly amazing, Jack! I have been around this game for a long time, and that is one of the greatest shots I have ever seen! I think that sets the stage for foundational principle four: **trust**."

Principle 4: Trust 

"Now this isn't a lecture, because as you stood there over your last shot, I heard what you said. You perfectly demonstrated this principle, though I could have gone without the cursing of the game after your first shot. After that, you had blind faith that if you just made your best swing the ball would make its way out of the woods. And it did!"

"Look, I agree that I have to do a better job of practicing religion, but I have never been one to bring God into the game golf."

"That is great, Jack, because the faith I am talking about has nothing to do with religious practices! The faith I am talking about is having an understanding and perspective that things happen for a reason in our life, both good and bad, and to *trust* that everything will work out. One of my favorite speeches is when Steve Jobs, the founder of Apple, is addressing a graduating class at Stanford, and he begins discussing how the dots are always connecting in your life, even if you don't realize it at the time. In his example, he randomly stumbled into a class about typography. Now he had no interest in typography prior to that, but after that class Steve was inspired to incorporate the different font styles into his first-ever computer. If Steve never wandered into that class, the creativity of the font styles in the first Apple computer would never have existed. You see, this principle isn't about maintaining your respective religious practice, this principle is about having faith and trust that the dots are always connecting in your life!"

The caddie continued with his lesson. "Let's look at this last hole, for example. You had a tough decision to make: driver or iron, and you went with what your intuition told you. That decision led to you hitting the ball into an almost-impossible lie, which had you questioning your decision and the moment in general. But something happened when you went to hit that shot. You trusted that if you gave it your best shot, literally and figuratively, it could turn out okay. Well, it turned out more than okay, Jack, you hit quite possibly the best shot of your life! You see, the dots were connecting in the background, even when you couldn't see it at that moment. The decision to go with the iron led to the shot into the woods, which led to an impossible lie, which led to one of the greatest shots I have ever seen. So when I talk about this principle of trust, I am talking about having trust in the grand scheme of things that the dots are always connecting in your life!"

"It really is wild to sit back and think about the ripple effects one moment, one decision, or one event can have on your life. I guess it has been hard for me to find that faith that everything happens for a reason. The decline in my sales, the increasing debt, the deteriorating relationship with my family. . . . I am not sure how those dots are connecting."

"Well, Jack, try to look it at this way. Maybe the decline in sales means you've maximized your potential in that career and you may have another calling out there to pursue. The increasing debt may help you realize there is more to life than possessions. Your family relationships are weakening perhaps because it is time for you to change your priorities. You see, we will never know how the dots will ultimately connect until later in life. That is the beauty of life: The possibilities are endless! But for you to live a meaningful life, you have to always have trust that every moment, decision, and event, both good and bad, are all connecting to complete your unique journey. Keep moving forward with positivity, and you will be amazed at the blessings you recognize that come your way. Now enough on this topic, I think you get the gist. Go knock that birdie in to capitalize on one of the greatest and most memorable shots you will ever have! A shot that wouldn't have been possible if you wouldn't have decided to hit an iron and had that bad shot into the woods off the tee!"

CHAPTER 10

The Strategy

"Another solid par, Jack. One more to go until the turn," the caddie said to Jack as they made their way to the ninth hole. The ninth hole was a classic Par 4, which entailed the most strategy of any hole on the course. It was a relatively large fairway, but fairway bunkers were prevalent along the middle portion of the hole. A good driver could hit over the bunkers, but a creek ran just around the 320-mark around the lofted green full of undulation and slopes. There was a reason it was a top-three hardest hole on the course—one that most amateurs would fall trap to.

As Jack stared at his course handbook, he noticed the traps all around him and every detail that was needed to have a successful hole. He had seen this type of hole before. He knew going for birdie would likely lead to a bogey, or worse. This was a hole that would require four perfectly executed shots just to walk away with par.

"I think I have my gameplan for this hole, Caddie, but you know this better than anybody. What do you think?"

"I think I absolutely love this hole because as the last hole on the front nine, it perfectly completes the five foundational principles that one must develop within to live a meaningful life."

"Well, what principle is that?"

"The foundational principle of **purpose**!" replied Caddie.

Principle 5: Purpose 

Purpose, huh? I sure have lacked a lot of that in my life lately, thought Jack to himself in his head. The caddie continued.

"Why I love this hole is that it requires a purposeful swing for every shot. If you just hit driver, chances are that it won't clear the creek and hit the hill in front and roll into the hazard. If you don't hit your iron in the right area and land in one of the fairway bunkers, you have a really tough chance of getting it on the elevated green in two with the water lurking in front. Let's say you are safe after your shot off the tee; you still have such a nasty green that if you land on one of the two downhill slopes, a two putt is almost impossible. Every shot requires purpose, just like life!"

"How does one find purpose in their life, Caddie? That's something that I feel has severely been missing in my life for some time. It's actually a question I have routinely asked myself regularly: What is my purpose?"

"First off, Jack—we don't *find* our purpose, we *create* our purpose! It seems these days, everyone is in some magical search to find their purpose. Now that isn't necessarily a bad thing; it is good that we want to find the reason why we are here. But if you get caught up in this constant search of finding your purpose, you are going to do more searching than actual living. Instead, you should take action and create your purpose in everything you do! Just like you need to embrace every moment, you also need to create purpose in every moment. Ultimately, you create and live your purpose through your everyday actions and attitudes."

"That is a great way of reframing the idea of purpose, Caddie. If I had a nickel for every time I asked myself what my purpose was the last five years, well, let's just say I wouldn't have the financial stress I do now," joked Jack. "But here I am no closer to the answer than I was five years ago!"

"Exactly, Jack! If you get caught up in the search for purpose, you will never actually live your purpose. You can create purpose in everything you do. You may not feel like your career is your life calling, and maybe it's not, but you can certainly create some type of purpose in your work. You create purpose through your family, your relationships, heck, you can even create purpose in how you interact with strangers."

"That all makes sense, but what if I can't create it? For instance, I've grown to dread my job. I don't know if it's because I'm not experiencing success anymore with it, if I have just burned out, or if I truly don't like it. Either way, I have been missing purpose in my career for quite some time."

"Well, when you first started, what was your *why* for becoming a salesman, Jack?"

"I guess I never thought about why I did it. The opportunity came along and I wanted to make some money. And when I started having lots of success, I liked the idea of the recognition I received and the ability to provide for my family."

"That makes sense. What would you say your purpose is now in that same role?"

"That's what I am getting at, Caddie! I don't think I have one! I'm miserable at work, and I continue to question why I even do this anymore. In fact, I think I've reached the biggest crossroads of my life—do I actually care if I get fired? Before today, I think I would have rather died than lose my position. But now I'm at a crossroad, perhaps the biggest crossroad of my life: Do I actually want my job? Or should I make a career change? Because finances aside, I don't actually see any purpose in my job. But I certainly need the income, and I'm not sure what else I would do. . ."

"This is an excellent example, Jack. In this scenario, you can decide that the question at hand is no longer suiting you to live your full purpose. If that is the case, then it is best to just move on. There is no shame in that. But before you do that, you must ask yourself if your *why* was for the right reason, or if you can reframe your purpose. For your current scenario, a lot of your original why and purpose has been for inherent selfish reasons. Maybe you can reframe your purpose to one of selflessness. Instead of viewing sales as dollar signs, view them as an opportunity to provide services or technology to help create a positive change on another business. Or view your role as a sales executive for your company as one that sustains and grows the revenue to allow your coworkers to have their jobs in other departments. It's been my experience that if you can reframe your purpose to one of selfishness to one of selflessness, then you will ultimately create a purpose worth living and sustaining!"

"That actually makes a lot of sense. I think back to when I was having the most fun and success, and that was when I truly enjoyed realizing the impact our product had on another business. Seeing how it affected lives for the better across the commercial relationships I made. I guess somewhere, through all the fortune and company fame, I lost that feeling."

"That is not abnormal at all, Jack. People stray from their purposes all the time. I have a little exercise that helps with that. But first, let's hit this tee shot. Remember, to go back to the golf analogy, if you were *searching* for the purpose of this tee shot, you would never realize the purpose. You would just stay standing looking at all the different options with no action. You see, the key to realizing your purpose is to create that purpose through action. Now create your purpose with this shot, commit to that purpose and take action on that purpose for this very shot."

"You got it, Caddie!"

Jack studied the hole once again. He knew this was a par hole, and the best way to make par was to hit a three wood over the bunkers and short of the creek. It would leave a long iron into the hole, but the purpose of this shot was to avoid all the traps and give himself a chance on his second shot to get to the green. As he stood over the ball, Jack mumbled to himself, "Commit to your purpose," and focused entirely on hitting the ball straight with the right distance. Sure enough, it landed precisely over the fairway bunkers and twenty yards shy of the creek. A perfectly executed purposeful shot!

"Way to go, Jack! Perfect!" the caddie shouted as they walked toward the fairway. I even heard you tell yourself to *commit to your purpose*, and that is exactly what you needed to do: keep that commitment to your why. We generally find ourselves in several roles in our adult life, perhaps if we are lucky enough even all of them. We are a lover, a parent, a friend, a professional, and an individual. Your aim should be to create purposes for each. To define how you can best love your significant other. To determine the type of role model you want to be for your children. To value your friendships and relationships. To find a deeper meaning in your work. And to embrace your uniqueness and things that make you happy. Once you have created purpose around those five roles, write them down on a notecard and carry it around in your wallet. When you feel like you are straying away from the purposes that *you created,* pull them out and remind yourself why you do the things you do in your life!"

"I guess I do wear a lot of different hats, don't I, Caddie. I tend to get caught up in one or the other, but all are equally as important. I have never really thought about all the different purposes I can have throughout my life. I always just thought about me and what I wanted to do."

"Exactly! This shot here is now its own unique shot with its own distinctive purpose. It serves a completely different purpose than the last shot. Remember why you are choosing to hit this unique shot (*choose* being the key word), then commit to taking action on that why!"

Jack turned his attention back to the ball. He could see the pin on the front left of the green. If he attacked the flag or the back middle of the green, both putts would be slippery downhill putts. But he noticed if he hit it short middle, he would leave himself with either a level putt or just off with a manageable chip to get up and down. Jack walked back to his bag and went one club lower. The purpose was to miss it short middle, as that would be much easier than any two putt on the left or back of the green closer to the actual hole. The caddie smiled as he saw Jack creating purpose with his shot—a shot that ultimately ended up landing in a great position just short of the green.

"Nice shot, Jack! Now that is hitting a golf shot with purpose! If you would have just gone up and hit your normal distance club, you likely would have found yourself in a really tricky situation. But you decided, again *decided*, to hit your shot with purpose, and look at the great result because of it. Everything you do in life matters, Jack, just like every golf shot in a round matters. You must create purpose in all you do, just like you must create purpose with every shot. Because if you don't, you may find yourself lost, drowning in the water, in over your head, buried in sand, or on a slippery slope with not a lot of options. Don't search for your purpose: create your purpose and fulfillment will find you!

CHAPTER 11

The Turn

"A par there is as good as gold, Jack. Nice purposeful playing," said the caddie after he rolled in his short par putt. Since he had left himself just short of the green in a safe place, Jack was able to easily pitch the ball within four feet of the hole for his par to cement an even score on the front nine. It was a really good score, all things considered, since Jack hadn't been actively playing for the last couple of years.

"What a front nine, Caddie! I think I've done more self-evaluation and learned more in the last two hours than I have the last two years! I'll take an even thirty-six on the front as well, let's see what we have in store on the back nine!"

"That was some really nice playing, Jack! And furthermore, hopefully you learned some things along the way to apply to your everyday life. What do ya think?"

"I think I had a lot of fun playing golf again, but that was exactly what I needed to hear! I haven't told you this yet, but there's a reason I decided to come here today after all this time. You see, I encountered a sign a few days back. As I was taking a walk after the worst day of my life I came across a white golf ball in the middle of an empty park. Golf is a part of who I am, and I knew it was a sign that I needed to go find myself on the course. I didn't anticipate my path coming across you though, but I sure am grateful that the dots connected me to you at this present moment to help me rediscover my purpose and prioritize balance in my life. You like what I did there?" laughed Jack.

"Very good," chuckled the caddie. "I was going to test you to see if you remembered, but looks like I don't have to! As we wrap up the front nine, I want to share a final note on the five principles we discussed. The principles of gratitude, presence, balance, trust, and purpose are foundational principles that you must develop at the core of your being. The reason they are foundational is they are bigger-picture principles that set the foundation on your journey through life. That foundation is appreciating all of life's blessings, and living in the only thing you actually have: the moment you are in. It means you're maintaining equilibrium through the different aspects of your life. You know and trust deep down that the dots will always connect. You're approaching everything you do with intention. You need to establish these principles as the foundation in all that you do to ultimately live a meaningful life and create fulfillment."

"I can absolutely see by even just adopting little aspects of each of these principles that they will fundamentally change my life for the better, Caddie! I'm confused on how to go about it, though. Does it just happen? What is the best way to start putting them to action?"

"Great question, Jack. It will take some time, and it won't be easy. But the more mindful you can become of establishing these as the foundation for your life, the more they will weave into the fabric of your being automatically. To establish the foundation, start by reflecting every morning and writing down something you are grateful for and the context to why. Every time you start drifting to the past or dreaming of the future, acknowledge it and then bring yourself back to be mindful of the present moment. Set governance to bring more balance, such as no work or cell phone between seven and nine p.m. to use that as family time. When something bad happens, remind yourself everything happens for a reason, and reflect on a time where you thought an event was unfavorable but ultimately became a blessing. Find the why in all that you do and try to look through a lens of selflessness when understanding that why. Take that why and create your purpose for all five of your roles. Remember, you ultimately get to create your purposes—don't search for them. By starting with these simple things across the five principles, you will over time build them into your foundation."

"Actionable ideas to live by these principles, I like it, Caddie! It is never too late to start. But is that it? We still have nine holes to play!"

"If only it were that easy, Jack! The five foundational principles are what we need to establish first, which is why I worked them into the front nine. The back nine will be mindset mantras. The foundational principles are higher-power values we use as the base to live by to serve a higher meaning. The mindset mantras are personal mindsets and actions that grow off the foundation that lead to self-realization and help keep you true to who you are. I'll work them in the back nine as I see fit. For now, go grab a quick hot dog and some water, and I will meet you over on the tenth tee. The journey of this round is just getting started, and hey, you still have a pretty decent chance at posting a low score." The caddie smiled.

Chapter 12

The Branch

As Jack stared down the tight fairway on the long Par 4 in front of him, he already felt like a changed man. He stood lighter on his feet, felt calmer in his heart, and had greater peace in his mind. It had been a long time since he had been in a place like that. He also had managed to get to the back nine at even par and felt excited about the potential of having a low score for the day. Due to the length of the hole, Jack knew he had to hit driver, but the trees along the fairway presented great trouble in the event of a poor shot. Jack let his driver rip with his perfect draw.

It looked good at first that it was going to draw left into the middle of the fairway right before it would meet the trees. But all of a sudden, the ball clipped the one branch hanging toward the fairway, and the ball fell down out of sight.

"No way that just happened. I hit that ball perfectly. How did it hit the one branch that could have impacted it!" screamed Jack.

The caddie observed Jack's body language change instantly. Jack went from a man of great contentment to fuming at the ears. "That is unfortunate, Jack. Perfectly striped ball, but sometimes those things happen. Nothing you can do about it now. Let's go see if we got a good bounce."

As Jack walked toward the trees his ball disappeared into, he couldn't believe that a ball hit that well could hit the one object that would impact it. Just when things were going well and he had reached a mental state he had not known for years, something like this happens. The more he thought about the unfortunate event, the more anger boiled up inside him. This wasn't his fault. He did his job and hit the ball perfectly. In his eyes, that branch should not even exist because it was clearly leaning out over the fairway. Someone else was responsible for this, not him. And he had to get that off his chest and say something.

"Why don't you trim your damn trees out of the fairway," muttered Jack to the caddie.

The caddie heard the words but chose to ignore them. He knew the feeling Jack currently had well. There is nothing more maddening when something bad happens to you that you perceived you had nothing to do with. But this was also a great lesson for the caddie's first mindset mantra. But before any lessons were going to be shared, he wanted to first see how this one would play out.

Jack agitatedly approached the trees to find his ball. As he scanned the area below the hanging branch, he finally saw the bad news. His ball had been plugged next to the tree. Not only would it take a good effort to get the ball out of the mud and into the fairway, he had to deal with the tree itself.

"Unbelievable! Are you kidding me? Of course it plugged straight down. Give me a wedge, Caddie, I guess I will just try to punch it out of here."

The caddie pulled the club from the bag, and Jack ripped it aggressively out of his hands. With little attention to detail, Jack went up to hack away as hard as he could. And the out-of-control swing caused him to get too underneath the ball, as it popped up and made its way about fifteen yards down the rough. He now laid two strokes and still had 175 yards to the tight green.

"Give me my seven iron, Caddie"

"You sure you don't want a six iron, Jack? That ball is covered in mud and the false front will bring the ball back down to the bottom of the hole."

"I know my distance. Give me the seven."

The caddie obliged and handed Jack the seven iron. By this time, Jack had completely lost his cool. With another rushed swing, Jack again had a poor result. The ball barely made the false front and trickled down the hill for another tough pitch onto the green.

"That's it! I am done! I should have just quit at nine while I was feeling good and ahead. This is an absolute joke. All because of one stupid branch hanging out over the fairway!"

The caddie, feeling the moment getting away from Jack, decided to pitch in.

"Jack. Remember foundational principle one."

"I do, Caddie. Are you telling me to be grateful for some tiny branch completely throwing off my game, my attitude, and my round?"

"No, Jack. While I think we can usually find gratitude in everything, life happens. Obstacles are thrown our way, and unforeseen events occur that we had nothing to do with. That's just part of life. To build on top of gratitude though, we must implement mindset mantra one: control what you can control.

Mindset Mantra 1: Control what YOU can control

"An event happens in one of two ways. You can either control it with some form of action or decision, or it simply just happens to you outside of your control. It's either one or the other. The foundation is to realize gratitude in the things that happen outside your control, both good and bad. But the real freedom you have in life is the ability to choose, not just the decisions you make when you have control, but also how you respond to events outside your control. If you can master the ability to learn that difference and respond with gratitude and understanding for the events outside of your control, you will ultimately find true contentment."

"That is all fine and good, Caddie. For me it isn't that simple. When I make a mistake or something bad happens based on my actions, that is on me. But when I do my part and the world continues to present bad luck, I am sorry but I just can't take it. This fire just burns inside of me that if I don't scream or hold someone else accountable, I feel like I might explode!"

"You are not alone, Jack. But unfortunate circumstances happen to all of us. I understand your frustration on hitting the branch, but really you are just out here playing a game for fun. Ultimately what it comes down to at the end of the day is perspective and a choice. What did that unfortunate event mean in the grand scheme of things, and how will you choose to respond to that event? Okay, so your ball hit a misplaced branch. Be grateful that you are still out here physically capable of playing good golf, and focus on what you can control: your mindset and perception of the event and what your next action is to make the best out of the situation!"

Jack took a deep breath to gather his thoughts. Though he was a man of great fortune and circumstances in his life, he would routinely get worked up over things outside of his control. He was allowing events outside his control to dictate his life.

"When I think back at all the things I have allowed to take control over me, instead of me taking control, it's pretty incredible how much stress and angst I could have avoided in my life. This might be the hardest mindset to develop by far as I've lived most of my life in reactive mode, allowing people and situations to influence my attitude and behavior. I can see by simply controlling what I can control that I can relieve much of the tension in my life. It seems simple, but how do you break a lifetime habit of allowing things outside your control to impact you?"

"It never is simple, Jack, and I'll let you in on a little secret: It will never be perfect. There will be moments when you'll react negatively to an event outside your control. You're only human, after all. But the more you can practice focusing on what you can control, you will see a big improvement on your overall well-being. The five mindset mantras I'm going to share with you build on the five foundational principles you just learned. For example, think about the foundation of gratitude. You practice gratitude to appreciate your blessings and look for the positive side of things out of your control. You then build off of that foundation to ultimately understand what is in your control—your attitude and mindset! You do not control branches on a golf course, or the weather, or how someone interacts with you, but you do control your attitude and how you respond. When you live with appreciation and understanding that the only thing you can control is your attitude, you take the first step to self-realization and living a fulfilling life with an attitude of gratitude!"

"Yeah, I always thought there was a lot of things in my control. I could control how I raised my kids, I could control my sales results, I could control my family finances. Now that I think about it, that isn't really the case. I cannot control the decisions of my kids—only my attitude in how I will raise them and support them on their decisions. I can't control whether my client actually signs the contract, but I can control my attitude toward them if they say no. I cannot control the inflow and inevitable outflow of money, but I can control my view of money and how it correlates to overall happiness. When it comes down to it, I guess the one thing we actually do control around the events in our lives is our attitude and how we *choose* to respond to them. And it is much easier to choose that mindset with an attitude of gratitude! Where did you learn all this, Caddie? This is some deep stuff!"

"Well, Jack, as you can see, I have learned a lot of these lessons the hard way, much like you. In golf, as in life, we can hit our shots into clean fairways as well as nasty roughs or hazards. I am always appreciative when I have the good fortune of having my ball land in the fairway. In the inevitable event when a ball lands in the rough, not only do I choose not to dwell on it, but I also choose to focus on what I can control for the next shot as the previous shot has already happened and been scored. There is a lot you can take from this great game of golf, Jack. For the ball not making the green, you have a pretty good angle there to get up and down and salvage a bogey. You aren't in such a bad position, after all. Now, what are you going to do?"

"Give me my sixty-degree wedge. I am going to do my best to control getting it on that back edge and let the rest take care of itself!"

CHAPTER 13

The Bogey Train

"Stay upbeat and positive, Jack. There's still a lot of golf to be played!" the caddie said to Jack as he put the eleventh hole flag back into the pin. Jack had salvaged a bogey on the tenth hole with a great pitch down the hill within four feet, but a three-putt on the eleventh was a very disappointing bogey to close it.

"Those are the type of holes you have to avoid! Three-putts like that can completely derail the round."

"Frustrating three-putt, no doubt, Jack. But stay in the moment; let's see how we can turn it around!"

Jack had calmed down significantly since his outbreak of rage on the tenth, but now his body language and mentality were turning more into despair. The caddie was trying to keep Jack upbeat with positive energy, but it was evident Jack had gotten into a little funk on this back nine. As they headed to the twelfth hole, a Par 3 over a tiny pond, the caddie sensed it was time to intervene, but he knew the moment would present itself when the time was right.

Jack grabbed his pitching wedge for the short Par 3 and slowly walked up to the ball. He couldn't get over the three-putt on the last hole. He had no one to blame but himself—that was certainly in his control—and it wasn't even that difficult to make par from where his approach landed. As he approached his ball, his mind clearly wasn't on the shot at hand nor was his energy at a place to make a great swing. As Jack took a soft swing with his wedge, it was no surprise to the caddie when it landed well right and short of the green. There was no outburst or words spoken by Jack this time, just a head down and a gentle walk to hit his next shot.

That next shot wasn't much better. The ball landed a good twenty feet right of the pin, leaving a very unlikely par putt. Jack would at least get that putt within five feet to two putts for a third consecutive bogey. All the life and energy that Jack had on the tenth tee was now nowhere to be found. In a matter of three holes Jack had a bogey due to unfortunate luck, a bogey due to his own bad putting, and a bogey due to sheer effort and not engaging in the moment. Jack grabbed his ball and silently and lifelessly proceeded to the easiest hole on the course, a short Par 5 that if executed correctly was a great chance at a birdie. The caddie knew now was the moment to get the round back on track and build off the foundation of the presence foundational principle to introduce the second mindset mantra.

The caddie grabbed the driver out of the bag to hand to Jack but held onto it to speak before presenting it to him. "Jack, before you hit this next shot, I want to remind you that you are on the thirteenth hole. You are not in a divot under a tree on ten, you are not missing a five-foot par putt on eleven, and we just left twelve behind us. Remember to attend to the present moment. That moment is this tee shot on the thirteenth hole, which just so you know is the perfect hole to go low and make up for some of the missed shots on the previous ones. Now lift that chin up, keep your head down, of course, and rip a drive down the middle of that fairway!"

Jack nodded. He knew he had lost focus on the moment and started feeling sorry for himself the last two holes. He also knew by looking at the downhill Par 5, he could definitely take advantage of this hole. He brought himself back to the present and told himself to focus on this one shot. Jack put a good swing onto the ball but just didn't hit it as flush as he wanted. The ball found the fairway, but about thirty yards shorter than what he was aiming for. He wasn't disappointed with the result, but Jack still walked toward the fairway with little pep in his step. The caddie knew what was missing.

"Jack, I could tell you that you brought yourself back to the moment, but if you really want to take the next evolution to self-realization, you just can't be in the moment, you have to live with enthusiasm for the moment. Which, coincidentally, is the second mindset mantra."

Mindset Mantra 2: Live with ENTHUSIASM for the moment

"Just like the last lesson, the "live with enthusiasm for the moment" mindset mantra builds on top of the foundational principle of presence. Enthusiasm is effectively the energy that you put out in this world. Enthusiasm is contagious. If you act with enthusiasm, you inherently spread that energy to those around you. And vice versa for negative energy. When you choose to be mentally present with enthusiasm, you live a happier and more fulfilling life. As Ralph Waldo Emerson said, 'Nothing great was ever achieved without enthusiasm.' Or also outlined by Jim Harbaugh, 'Every day and every moment is an opportunity to attack the day with an enthusiasm unknown to mankind.'"

Jack understood. His current life was devoid of enthusiasm and was full of dreaded dull. When he woke up in the morning, the first emotion he felt was dread. He dreaded having to go to work and face his colleagues, bosses, and the few prospects he had. With no energy to draw inspiration from, his days grew dull, just counting the time down to go home. It was a vicious cycle, one that had compounded over the last few years, leaving Jack feeling angry, negative, and lifeless. A man once admired for his great energy and passion for life was now someone not even his family wanted to be around. When it came to this, Jack's problem was deeper than just not being in the moment: it was the enthusiasm-less void he had been living in the last few years.

The caddie continued, "I know you have it in you, Jack. If you were great at sales, then I know you naturally had great enthusiasm, because sales ultimately is the transfer of enthusiasm from one person to another! I do not know the inner workings of your life, but it could be that the more you lived with negativity and lack of energy, the fewer sales you made. Enthusiasm is a pivotal aspect in anything that we do. And the best way to draw enthusiasm is to be truly present and enjoy the moment."

"You know what, Caddie. When I think back on the last couple years of failure in my job and unhappiness in my life, it can be traced back to losing that zest for life in what I was doing at that point. When I was having success in sales, I truly enjoyed those moments presenting in a board room and establishing great commercial relationships. When I would come home, I loved going to my son's practice and taking part in his development. At some point, I began worrying about things unforeseen, taking my attention away from the moment and ultimately my enthusiasm for it. Relaxing Sundays with my family quickly turned into stressful days worrying about all I had to do on Monday. I can now see that the root of my problems was not only staying present, but it was that lack of presence that eroded my enthusiasm over time. When things were going well, I would say enthusiasm was one of my defining characteristics. Now I can see it is that the lack of enthusiasm I have is directly causing unhappiness in my career, my family, and my life.

"Well, Jack, that's what happens when you get caught up in the past or start worrying about the future: You lose enthusiasm for the actual present moment. You can use the past for lessons learned, and it is certainly important to prepare for the future, but all we really have in this life is that present moment. To quote a line from the movie *Any Given Sunday* in his famous 'Inches' speech, Al Pacino passionately tells his team, 'That's what living is, the six inches in front of your face!' I do not know of any truer words. When it comes down to it, those six inches in front of our face are all that we have at that moment. So why not enjoy it with enthusiasm?"

"Yeah, I guess that has been one of my greatest flaws as of late. My mind is always racing about the past or guessing the future that it takes up so much energy that I cannot concentrate on having great energy in the moment."

"It's a hard habit to break. Take for example the last couple holes. When you missed that five-foot par putt on the eleventh hole, you completely lost all your positive energy. When we stood on the tenth tee, you were ready to conquer the world. After some tough luck and a bad putt, in the matter of two holes you were back to feeling sorry for yourself. Let me let you in on a little secret: shit happens. It happens to all of us. But you have to keep moving forward with positive enthusiasm. Your attitude and lack of energy led to that bogey on twelve. Not a branch, not your putting stroke, but your inability to focus on the moment at hand with positive energy. You let the outcomes on the last two holes dictate your attitude and energy on the hole you were actually on. My guess is that is what happened to your life. It is a hard reality to face. But if you learn to focus on your presence and live with that enthusiasm for the moment, I am positive that you will live a happier and more meaningful life."

"You're completely right, Caddie. These last three holes are indicative of my life recently. I guess when the shit happens, it completely draws me away from the moment. It has been for years. The worry, negativity, doubt all creep into my mind, and my energy is pulled away from truly enjoying and living in the moment. This has compounded over so many years—how can I just recreate my everyday enthusiasm?"

"Great question, Jack. There are two ways you can start drawing enthusiasm in the moment. The first is to get back to doing what you love and brings you joy. For example, this great game of golf. Commit to playing one a week. Turn your phone off, don't worry about your score, and just stay in the moment and enjoy this amazing game. Make commitments to grab dinner with your kids and be fully there and enjoy the conversation and the amazing things that come with being a father. Take your wife out on some dates and keep your phone off in your pocket. Life is too short not to do what we love. But we all know that not everything we do in life is out of love. There are inevitably going to be times when we aren't enjoying that moment. But the beauty is that we get to decide that! If you start feeling down or void of enthusiasm for the moment, choose to be *enthusiastic!* We literally have the power to use our minds to act with enthusiasm. Thus, the second way is when you don't have it in the moment, just force yourself to act enthusiastic and you will ultimately *be* enthusiastic. As a salesman, I am guessing you may have read Frank Bettger's book on how he became a great sales professional from his early failures. The one thing he said he learned that completely changed his results was to act with enthusiasm, even when he didn't want to. He forced himself to live with enthusiasm, and in turn he actually did—which led to great results in his professional and personal life."

The message was starting to resonate with Jack. He saw a path forward out of the dreaded dull he had been living with for years. The life began to come back into Jack's mind, body, and spirit.

"Let's try it right now," said the caddie. "I'll show you the power firsthand. Bring yourself back to the moment, this second shot on the Par 5. Due to a short drive, it's going to be tough to get it on in two. But if you hit it flush with some juice, you can make it happen. That's our present reality. Now tell your mind to have enthusiasm with this shot. Not many people could get it on in two from here. That's an exciting challenge. Feel the energy rushing through your body. Feel the enthusiasm for this game, for this life, for this moment. What a moment it is! Be enthusiastic for this shot, because that ball is the six inches in front of your face!"

Jack nodded in approval. He stared at the challenge in front of him and told himself to be excited for this challenge. As the mind did its magic, Jack felt energy pulse through his veins. He was back in the moment. After one final look at the long stretch of grass ahead of him, Jack turned to the caddie and said confidently, "Let's do this!"

The caddie could feel the positive energy circulating in the air. He saw his player not only living in the present but buzzing with enthusiasm for the moment. Jack took a few practice swings to get his body loose for the power he knew he would have to generate. He took one final deep breath before he addressed the ball to let it rip. There was no worrying about past misfortunes and mistakes or looking forward at the challenge with dread. It was just Jack, the ball, 250 yards of grass, and a burning enthusiasm for the greatness of this moment.

Chapter 14

The Decision

"Good things can happen when you live with enthusiasm. Great eagle, Jack!"

Jack had just buried his five-foot eagle putt after one of the best shots he had ever pulled off in his life. With the sense of living in the moment pulsing through him, Jack absolutely stung his approach. He caught a little luck when it struck the top of a bunker and popped up to hit the downslope then softly rolled within five feet. It was the perfect moment to show the power of enthusiasm, and Jack's great round was back on track.

"I couldn't have made that shot without you! I don't know how you know when to pull the right strings, but I sure am glad you are on my bag today! Back to one over, let's see if we can get it to even."

"Let's see what we can do. It is going to be hard on this upcoming hole, though. Fourteen is a long and tricky dogleg right with thick rough and plenty of fairway bunkers," the caddie said to Jack as they made their way to the next hole.

Jack surveyed the different options. He could try and blast it to the right and perhaps clear the trees, but if he didn't hit it perfectly he would leave himself with a horrible angle or even worse—dead into the woods. He could keep it to the left, and a three wood would leave him short of the fairway bunker with a long approach but a great angle. It was a golfer's hole, and Jack's renewed life had him enjoying the decision.

The caddie saw Jack playing through the options and decided to step in. "I know you can see the options. But you are playing with fire if you decide to take it on and try to clear the trees. Guaranteed bogey if you don't make it. The left keeps you in play but leaves a challenging approach. Either way, commit to the decision."

Jack was feeling confident and cocky after that last shot, so he grabbed the driver. If he could get ahold of it again and clear the trees, he was looking at an easy wedge into the green to give himself a birdie and a chance to get back to even. As he took one final survey of the hole, he started approaching the ball. But once he got to the tee and made one last final glimpse before him, he took a step back and retreated.

"You're right . . . Big risk and reward taking that on. No need to throw the round away now. Let me see that wood."

The caddie handed Jack the three wood. He knew Jack was making the right decision, but he could also sense the non-committal shot Jack was about to take. Jack's mind was telling him to go with the smart play of the three wood. Jack's heart was telling him to let it rip and to go for it. Being in-between your mind and your heart is never a good thing and creates unhealthy tension. However, in this case, the tension was already there, so the caddie let the scenario play out. And as he expected, Jack never truly committed to the shot, which resulted in him getting underneath the ball for a short drive and an even longer approach.

"I knew I should have hit the driver, I knew it! A two-hundred-yard drive isn't going to help me one bit. I should have gone with the driver like my heart told me."

"Well, therein lies your problem, Jack. You never committed to the shot. How are you supposed to execute the shot if you can't commit to it? I observed you going through the options, and I could sense the questioning. The smart move was clearly going with the wood to keep it in play, but your heart was telling you to let it rip with the driver. If your heart is pulling you one way and your mind the other, you will not be able to fully hit the shot you end up choosing. This happens regularly not only in golf but in life. When you make a decision, you need to completely commit to that decision as well. Which leads me to mindset mantra three that builds off the foundational principle of balance: Always be committed and consistent in your decisions.

Mindset Mantra 3: Always be committed and consistent in your decisions

The caddie continued, "This mindset builds off balance because to live with balance, you must be able to consistently commit to it. Take your last shot, for example. Your head was pulling you one way and your heart was pulling you the other. It threw off your mental and spiritual balance. With that imbalance and lack of commitment to a decision, the result almost always ends up just like your last mediocre shot. Let's look at some real-life examples. If you make a goal to lose weight and live a healthier lifestyle but only commit to dieting and exercising half of the time, you will only see mediocre results. If you want to start saving toward a specific financial goal but only commit to putting half of the money in, you will only reach half of the savings target. You see, we must fully commit to whatever endeavor we have in front of us and then consistently take action."

"Yeah, well, commitment is hard. When I look at the imbalance in my life between my work and my family, I would always make a commitment to spend more time with them or not be on my phone. That may work for a week or two, but I would almost always fall back into the same habits. How do you maintain that commitment?"

"You're right, Jack, commitment is hard! It may be one of the hardest areas to master, because as you stated, it is easy for us to fall back into our bad habits that disrupt our balance. The best way to develop commitment to a certain goal or decision is consistency. As a person in sales, I know you likely know the ABCs of sales to get to the successful outcome of a sale is to "Always Be Closing." Well, think of this mindset mantra to get to certain successful outcomes in your life as the ABCDs of living. We make small and big decisions daily. The key is being intentional in making decisions that align with your core commitments you have made to yourself and others and then commit to making them consistently. Commitment and consistency go hand-in-hand."

The caddie and Jack arrived at Jack's short drive. As Jack surveyed the options, he had another tough golf decision to make: Hit a long iron layup and leave himself with a gap wedge to try and get up and down, or try to sting a fairway wood and get enough on it to reach the green but with enough touch to keep it on. Again, Jack's heart was telling him to go for it, but his mind was telling him to play it safe.

"Well, God has a funny way of teaching his lessons. Here we are again, another tough decision. What will it be?"

"I know, I was just thinking that. Exact same scenario. My heart is saying go for it. My mind is telling me to hit a great layup, just like my tee shot. To your earlier point, how do you know what the right decision is when your heart and mind conflict?"

"That is a great question. If I knew that answer, I probably wouldn't be a caddie," the caddie joked. "But in all seriousness, you never really know the right decision until after it has been made. When it comes to a decision, you take in all the external and internal factors. Water to the left, trees to the right. The smart play is to layup, the hero in me wants to go for it. There is always a lot to consider. Sometimes it is an easy decision, but most of the times you face this very conflict you do now. In my experiences, if your heart is about to explode out of your chest because you feel so strongly about the decision, then just do it! The heart almost never leads us wrong, and we generally feel no regret if we go with our heart. Other times, we can rely on past experiences and knowledge to just know that our logical mind is making the right decision. But the best advice I have in these situations is that when the decision is made, you fully commit to it and never look back. Again, you never know how the dots will connect. Commit to the decision and drive that commitment with consistent action!"

Jack nodded to the caddie, knowing his action would speak louder than words. He studied the lie of his ball and noticed that the high drive caused a bit of a plug. He almost always wanted to go for it in these situations; that is how Jack played golf. But through years of playing the game since a little kid, he also knew that to get it there he would have to hit the ball perfectly with this fairway wood and that would not be possible with his current lie. His heart always wanted to be the golf hero, but sometimes you need to rely on experience and logic to make a decision. Jack turned toward the caddie.

"Give me my five iron. Let's try to keep it in play and give ourselves a good angle in."

The caddie nodded and handed the five iron to Jack. He knew it was the right decision, and Jack delivered by hitting it perfectly and leaving himself about ninety yards into the green for his third shot.

"Well done, Jack. I watched you go through your options, and you clearly made the right decision. More importantly, you had conviction in your decision and committed to that shot. Your body language spoke it as much, way more than your hesitant tee shot."

"Thank you for the lesson, Caddie. Crazy how confident your swing feels when you truly commit to your decision."

"It makes all the difference! Furthermore, your decision was an impressive one. In this game, almost everyone wants to go for the great shot. But it makes me think back to one of the greatest feats this game has ever seen: the 2019 Tiger Woods victory at The Masters on the iconic Par 3 twelfth hole. Two of the players in front of Tiger's final pairing had just attacked it dead at the pin and left it short, and the ball rolled back into the creek. The well-ahead leader had the honors and couldn't resist for going at the flag. I mean who wouldn't want to make an incredible shot on the grandest stage at its most legendary hole? But he also found the creek, leaving the door open for Tiger. But instead of Tiger making his typical heroic and unforgettable shot, he used decades of experience on that course to know the right play was to play it well left and just get it on the green to give himself a chance at par. It was that commitment to make the right decision and that par that kept him alive in the tournament, and it wasn't too long before he hunted down the lead and completed his greatest masterpiece. Now knock this wedge within five feet, Jack. The golfing energy usually rewards smart, committed shots."

Jack smiled and confidently stepped up to his ball and hit it with perfect touch to get the ball within four feet of the hole. A par the hard way, but a par that illustrated the power of a committing to a consistent and disciplined decision. With four holes to play, Jack had the opportunity to shoot one of the greatest rounds of his life.

CHAPTER 15

The Sand

"Back to even, Caddie! I can't believe I have a chance to shoot below par my first time back in years!" Jack shouted after rolling in a ten-foot birdie on the Par 3 sixteenth.

"You have really bounced back since the struggles to start the back nine. It is a long round, and you stayed with it and are making some incredible golf shots. There are still two holes to go though, so let's stay in the moment."

Jack walked up to the seventeenth hole, a straight and narrow Par 4 lined heavily with fairway bunkers. He breathed deeply to take in the scene as he couldn't believe the position he was in. Jack hadn't golfed regularly in years, let alone shoot below par like he could every once in a while back in his prime. Overall, he knew this round had been more about the final score, but he also wanted deeply to finish into negative numbers. He'd had a rough go lately, and this was a much-needed break from life. *And let's face it,* he thought, *I may not have much more golf to play if my condition takes a turn for the worst.*

"Just hit it straight here, Jack. No need to try and drive it, I think a three wood or long iron would do. We just want to avoid those bunkers as hitting from that sand will make it tough to get there in two."

Jack nodded and grabbed his long iron out of the bag. He wanted to try and hit a stinger shot and let the ball run down the fairway. But as he tried to sting it, his body got ahead of him and caused him to hit the ball a bit left. "Stay short of that bunker. Don't roll in, ball," Jack was imploring to himself as the ball tracked right toward the bunker. But Jack had gotten some juice on it, and the ball had too much motion on it as it rolled into the deepest of the fairway bunkers.

"Well, that is golf for ya. Those things happen. Let's go check the lie and see if we can get it out of there to the green," said the caddie.

As they made their way to the bunker, Jack's intuition was unfortunately correct. It was not pretty. The ball must have kicked off the front lip and plugged deeply into the slope on the face of the bunker. There would be no chance of getting it remotely close to the green, and just getting out in general would be a success at this point. As Jack examined his ball, he knew the only play was to just pitch it out of the bunker and into the fairway. He grabbed his seven iron and made his way into the pit of sand.

While standing over his ball, the top lip of the bunker started to intimidate Jack. *Can I really get that over that lip with a seven?* Jack thought to himself.

He tried judging the lie of the ball and whether a seven iron would have enough degree to get it out. As he squared up to get a feel for his shot, he grounded his club into the sand just behind the ball and caused the ball to roll back into a much cleaner lie.

"Dang it," Jack muttered under his breath. He knew he had just broken one of golf's sacred rules in that you can't ground the club into the sand to creative an advantage for the shot. The ball had barely moved, and it wasn't like he was playing for money or in a competitive tournament. He took a step back to recompose himself and looked over at the caddie, who was watching an eagle soaring in the sunlit sky. Jack knew the caddie was a golf purest and would call him out on it, but determined there was no way he had seen the penalty. Now that he could get to the back of the ball cleanly, he proceeded with his seven iron and had a perfect long out that left him a wedge out in the middle of the fairway.

What Jack didn't think of was that the caddie knew this course better than anyone, and that he also knew that with the plugged lie on the slope Jack had that not even some of the best players in the world could have caught it cleanly like he just did. Though he did not directly see Jack ground the club, he got the sense from Jack's initial reaction and the shot itself that Jack had used a penalty to his advantage. Nevertheless, the caddie wasn't there to keep score and he wanted to see how Jack would respond.

As soon as Jack had hit his shot, he was overcome with guilt. Jack was raised to play this game the right way with the proper etiquette and the respect for the rules. But clashing with the guilt in his gut was also the excuses in his head. *Not taking a stroke penalty isn't going to affect anyone. This is a leisure round; everyone gets a mulligan. If you take the two-stroke penalty now, you can absolutely kiss goodbye to the chance to finish under par, so just let it slide.* But again, his heart was fighting his mind. *You know the penalty provided you with an advantage, thus you have to do the right thing and take the penalty. Will you ever be fully happy and accomplished knowing the final score of this round is a fraud?*

Jack didn't know what to do. In the grand scheme of things, not taking the penalty would have no negative impact on anyone else's life. He wasn't stealing money or a championship, and he wanted to play the eighteenth hole with a chance to shoot under par. But he also knew the right thing to do was to take the penalty on this hole, as that is what he ultimately deserved. He didn't want the caddie to sense his inner conflict, so he hit his relatively easy approach shot rather quickly and hit it to within six feet. If he made this putt and didn't take the stroke penalty, he would have a chance to birdie the final hole to meet his end goal.

There was no fooling the caddie though, and by observing Jack he now concluded what had happened. To truly test Jack, he decided to put it out there to see what Jack would do.

"All right, Jack, pretty straight putt for par here. Make this and you have a chance to birdie the last and get it to red numbers. Knock it in, baby!"

As Jack went through his pre-putt routine analyzing the break and feel of the putt, his heart had now clearly overpowered his mind. A final score for the round meant nothing if he didn't do it the right way. That much he knew through all the lessons and principles he had learned up to this point. He stepped away from the ball and responded to the caddie.

"Actually, Caddie, I am going for a double bogey here. When I was deciding which club to hit out of the bunker, I took my seven iron to judge the angle and test the sand and ended up grounding the club to the sand and creating a cleaner lie for my ball. By my calculations, the two-stroke penalty has me lying five. Originally, I didn't want to say anything as that significant of a penalty would ruin my chance at breaking par. But golf is not a game you cheat, no matter what the circumstances. Thus, I am taking the penalty as I created an advantage with the grounding of my club."

"Jack, that took a lot of accountability to admit that and take on the penalty yourself. To be honest, I didn't directly see you do it, but from experience I knew you likely did something to enhance the lie. I am proud that you have admitted to your penalty—and even more because you unwittingly passed the test of exhibiting the next mindset mantra: Do the right thing, even when nobody is watching. This builds off the foundational principle of trust."

Mindset Mantra 4: Do the right thing, even when nobody is watching

The caddie continued, "Doing the right thing, even when nobody is watching, is a key mindset because it ultimately drives you to live a life of integrity. Integrity is the truthfulness of one's actions. Essentially, we live with integrity if through our every action and decision we are demonstrating our core values and these very principles. Doing the right thing with integrity builds off of the personal principle of trust because you must have trust that the dots will always connect when you make decisions that align with your values, even if that decision may hurt you in the short-term. Take for example this stroke penalty. No one was watching, and you could have easily not taken the penalty to give yourself a chance at your ultimate goal. But you had trust in your decision to take the penalty, as the consequences of not being truthful—and the consequences of not living with integrity—would have outweighed the short-term satisfaction you could have gained."

"It is funny you say that, Caddie, because lately I haven't been a man of much integrity. Everything I do is a short-term benefit to me personally. Whether that be pressuring a client to a new sale when I know we haven't covered key details, or escaping my family duties to go drown my anxieties in the bottle. I really didn't think about the long-term aspects of my decisions because I never had any faith that things would ultimately work out. I can see how integrity builds off of trust, because if I trust that doing the right thing will benefit me in the long-term, then I can make integrity-based decisions and actions."

"Exactly, Jack! Look at you, I didn't even have to teach you this time. To me, being a man of integrity consists of three things. One, do my decisions and actions align with my core principles and values? Two, do I trust that by making the right decisions or doing the appropriate actions will benefit me and the others around me in a positive way in the long-term? Three, and maybe most importantly, if my decision or action were to be broadcast to the world, would I be representing myself and my family in a way to make them proud?"

"Those are great ways to look at it. Can you expand more on the final item? That is a powerful statement."

"Agreed, I personally believe the last is the most profound. We are all faced with questionable decisions or bad habits that drive distasteful actions, oftentimes in the solitude of our lives where no one is watching. That is part of being a human. We tend to make those decisions and engage in those bad habits out of our own desires and interests. We rarely think about how those decisions and actions could affect our family, friends, and loved ones. Thus, the best way to live with integrity in your everyday decisions and actions, is to think about those that matter most. The easiest way to visualize this is to imagine you are in the heart of Times Square in New York City with your family, surrounded by giant, flashing billboards. On the billboard directly in front of you, your decisions and actions are being played on repeat for your whole family to see. How does that video make them feel? Does it shame them? Does it change the way they see you? Or does it make them proud and want to be better? If it's the latter, then you can be confident in knowing that you are living with integrity."

"That is an incredible perspective, Caddie, and certainly captures the power of that statement. In regard to the penalty, I was raised on a certain set of golf values from my father. He always preached to play the game the right way, and the game will reward you. When I admitted to the penalty, it was more that I knew I didn't want this amazing round to be a fraud—a principle my father instilled in me. But another way I could have looked at it as well is: How would my father have thought of me if I decided to cheat the game to save two strokes? What would my family see if they saw me ground the club but not take responsibility for it? It is a great mindset to live life by: Doing the right thing, even if no one is watching. Because deep down, I know that by not living with integrity I'm cheating myself and the ones that matter most."

"You got it, my man! And to answer your question, your dad would have been proud . . . as am I. You're starting to see the bigger picture, Jack! But we aren't finished yet. There's one more hole to goal, and hey, two over heading to the final hole isn't too shabby either. Your growth during this round has been impressive. Now let's finish it off strong!"

"You got it, Caddie!" Jack smiled. He felt much lighter after his decision to take the penalty, and he had a sense of calm and peace to him that it would all work out.

Success = Impact

As Jack surveyed the final hole, a beautiful Par 4 with an elevated tee shot, he reflected on what a life-changing round he just played while admiring the beauty of the bird's-eye course around him. The round had had its normal swing of circumstances and outcomes. There were moments and shots Jack would never forget. But the main thing that stood out in his mind above all else was the incredible man alongside him that had impacted his perspective on life in the four short hours he had known him. He almost couldn't believe it and for a moment questioned whether this was all a dream. But then, remembering how this all started with finding a golf ball in a park, he realized that God must have put the caddie in his life—when he least expected it.

"Caddie, I just want to say thank you for everything you did over the round. I can definitely say it has already helped change my life. I know I still have a lot to work on, but the lessons, principles, and mindsets you provided have pointed me in the right direction and were exactly what I needed to hear. It's funny because when I came across the golf ball a few days ago, I thought the energy of the universe was telling me I would find myself and the answers to my questions by coming back to the game of golf. I wanted to play this round by myself with no one but me. I can now see that it wasn't golf the world was connecting me to—it was you!"

"I appreciate that, Jack. This is why I love golf so much. It affords me the opportunity to connect with other people as well as use this great game and its little intricacies to teach how to live a meaningful life. Without meaning or purpose, we will never be truly happy or realize why are here to begin with."

"Absolutely," agreed Jack, "and it hits home even more that you used my favorite game and passion to teach me the principles and mindsets that I needed to hear. One other thing on purpose, though. I know purpose is the last foundational principle, and with this being the last hole, I assume we will have one mindset mantra left that builds on purpose?"

"That's correct, Jack."

"Well, before you surprise me with more wisdom. I've been thinking about purpose a lot, even before all the events happened recently. Like, what was my purpose? Was I really meant to be a great salesman? Is there something else I should be doing? Is there more to life? I know you say to create our purpose across the different aspect of our lives, but I don't even know where to start. I'm forty-five years old. I can't just up and quit my job and do something different. I have a mortgage and bills to pay, so how else do I create my purpose?"

"First, Jack, your career doesn't have to be your one and only purpose. Some people are lucky in that their career is also their calling and highlights their gifts. But most people have to find avenues outside their career to create their purpose. There is not one size that fits all when it comes to creating and living out your purpose."

"Yeah, I guess I have always tied my profession and work to my purpose. But where do I even begin? I know deep down I'm not realizing my true self. But what my true self is, I really don't know."

"That, my friend, is where the final mindset mantra comes into play. Before we discuss it though, I think you should tee off. Put one last good drive into play and let's see how we can finish this great round out."

Jack grabbed his driver and winked at his new friend as he took his stance. There was no doubt in Jack's swing as he swung with rhythm, command, and purpose. The ball jumped off his driver and landed perfectly in the left of the fairway with a great angle to the pin in the back right of the green. As they started making their final walk of the day, the caddie continued his wisdom.

"Jack, you want to know where to begin to create your purpose? Take this fifth mindset mantra to heart and you will create a life of purpose and fulfillment in all that you do: Success equals Impact!"

Mindset Mantra 5: Success = IMPACT 

"Any purpose that carries any meaning must be rooted in the ability to positively impact others. We will never live a life of fulfillment if our purpose is self-centered. We live with fulfillment when we make an impact on this world. The beauty is you don't have to be a millionaire or a celebrity to make this type of impact. Those generally get celebrated more, but you can make a positive impact every day. You can impact your family, your friends, your coworkers, and even complete strangers you didn't even know four hours ago." The caddie smiled.

Jack stood quiet for a few moments. "Maybe that is why I've had such a hard time discovering or creating my purpose . . . because everything I've done the last decade has been all about me: my successes, my financial gain, my pleasure. It makes sense that I feel so empty and devoid of meaning, because I have only cared about what positively impacts me."

"That could certainly be why," replied Caddie. "I mean, look how society paints our vision of success. Success defined in society's terms is usually judged by the size of your bank account, the type of car and house you own, or personal achievements and rewards. Those things are all great, and I am not saying you shouldn't want to have financial security, a great lifestyle, and personal accomplishments. What I am saying is that if at the very core your desires and actions are to gain the superficial success only for yourself, then you are not truly living a successful and fulfilling life. Actual success is realized when you make a positive impact on others."

Jack now fully understood why his life felt so empty. For years his sales efforts were all about him. They weren't about the success of his clients; they were the check that went into his bank account. He remembered his early days when from a success standpoint he was the number one rep in his company; he truly cared about this clients and partners. It was why his customers loved him so much and continued to buy from him. During that same time period, he always made it a point to be at his son's baseball practice or spend quality time with his wife and family. Along the way, he lost caring about those around him and started caring more about himself. Now, not only wasn't he accomplishing the "superficial" success of money and accomplishments, he had zero meaning to his life. And that essentially stemmed from the lack of impact he was making on others.

The caddie continued after giving Jack a moment to himself and almost reading his mind. "In more instances than not, the money, the recognition, the applause—they are a natural byproduct when at your core you are living to impact others. The energy around us rewards those who create a purpose of serving and impacting others. If you start with that, the rest of the stuff somehow follows. But true happiness and fulfillment doesn't come from the stuff. It comes from deep relationships and positively impacting this world. And if you think about it, what constitutes a successful golf shot?"

"A good golf shot, depending on when it takes place, is keeping it straight within the fairway or hitting the green close to the pin."

"Interesting answer," replied Caddie. "And I guess, on a superficial level, you are right about that. You are right that it really depends on when the shot is taking place, as there are a lot of shots within golf that can qualify as great shots. But there is one commonality that all great shots have in common. You know what that is, Jack?"

"No, what?"

"All great golf shots are a result of the club making perfect *impact* with the ball. That is the true essence of golf. When the human and club in harmony make synchronous impact on the ball. As a golfer, you know the instance it happens. There is no other feeling like it in the world. Just pure, beautiful impact. When it comes down to it, that is what golf is. Whether it be a driver, iron, wedge, or putter, it is all about using the tools and gifts you have to make perfect impact on that ball. The same is true in life. That is why I love this game so much. There are so many similarities in the game of golf that align with the game of life. But at the very foundation of both, it comes down to one simple concept: making positive impact. That's all it is."

Jack was speechless. All these years, he had never thought about golf or life like that. There were so many lessons throughout this round, but now it finally made sense. All the principles and mindsets matter, but if there was one thing he could take away, it was this mindset right here. He needed to reframe how he looked at everything. From his career to his relationships and heck, even the game of golf. He was so deep into his self-reflection that he almost forgot they still had the final hole to play.

"Remember this feeling," implored the caddie. "I know deep down that you are a man with great influence. You mean well and you have a good heart. It can be easy to lose track of that during certain seasons of life. But hold on to this moment. And whenever you feel lost again, just remember this concept. We try to complicate both life and golf with all this noise around us, but when it comes down to it, the meaning of life and the game of golf isn't that hard to understand. Just make a positive impact in all you do. On this upcoming shot, on all shots in the future, and to all those around you."

Jack nodded to the caddie. There was nothing else to say. Only action and mindset here on out would prove if Jack would take this to heart. But Jack finally had the answers to his questions he had been asking himself over the last couple of years. He didn't know what awaited him after this hole, but he knew what he had to do to finally embrace looking himself in the mirror again. Seeing the reality facing him and the major mental challenges and changes he would have when he would walk off the eighteenth green to back up what he learned with action, he tried bringing himself back to the moment. He silenced his mind on what he would do in the future and forgot about all the mishaps in the past and brought himself to be one with himself, the club, and the ball like he used to when he was a little boy. "Just make a positive impact on the ball, Sonny," he quietly told himself.

With his only focus on making positive impact, Jack made that pure contact that every golfer dreams about. The caddie watched in awe at the beautiful ball flight as the ball soared into the blue sky and down to the green while landing softly on the top middle ridge that sent it rolling down to the back-right pin. They both looked in increased excitement and amazement in the distance as the ball kept rolling and tracking right at the stick until the white ball disappeared from the line of sight.

CHAPTER 17

The Why

Jack started walking briskly to the green to see what happened. He wanted to enjoy the walk on his final hole, but he couldn't contain his excitement as he made his way up the hill to the green to see if what he was thinking indeed did occur. "Did that go in, Caddie? Talk about impact! I struck that thing so clean. I can't see it up there."

"From my vantage point, I saw it hit the perfect spot but lost sight when it made its way toward the back right near the pin."

The men approached the green like little kids on Christmas. When they finally made their way up there, there was no ball on the green. The pair looked at each other simultaneously and smiled.

"Go check it out, Jack. You either hit the shot of your life or that ball is somewhere off the green. Let's hope for the first, though!"

Jack made his way to the hole, but this time he slowed his approach. With every step he thought about his entire journey that had led him to this moment. From the early days of playing golf with his dad every day to the struggle of having to cut his dream of playing professionally short due to injury. Then, he was re-invigorated by a new challenge and career in enterprise sales and all the personal and monetary success that came with it. Finally, his mind cut to the last few years that had been filled with emptiness and disappointment. He thought about how a lot of his life was similar to this incredible round he just played, with many Fairways as well as several Bunkers, and a whole lot of lessons along the way. He finally arrived at the hole and looked down to see the number two ball looking back at him exactly as it did in the park just a few days prior! Jack smiled to himself and felt that innate peace we all desire.

"Well, Jack?"

Jack reached into the cup and pulled out his ball and let out a big fist pump with ball in hand toward the caddie and screamed, "Let's go! An eagle for an overall round of even Par!"

The caddie couldn't believe it. What a culmination to one of the more enjoyable rounds he had ever been a part of. He was so excited that he ran over to Jack and gave him a big hug. Four hours ago, they were total strangers, now they were bonded in each other's unique stories forever.

Jack guided the caddie off the green toward a set of trees to have a moment to gather himself and get closure on one of the best and most important rounds of his life. "Caddie, I just want to say thank you for everything this entire round. The golf aspect was fun and great, but all the lessons of the foundational principles and mindset mantras were exactly what I needed to hear. I had lost my way in life. I understand this now and know the principles I need to apply, along with the mindsets that I can personally control. I know it will be a lot of work and I have much to change, but at least now I know a lot of the issues and lack of meaning in my life. All this time, I thought that God was leading me to find myself in the game of golf, but now I realize he was leading me to you to use the game of golf to change my life. And for that, I am forever grateful."

"Jack, I honestly appreciate the kind words, and as much as you say I have impacted you, the truth is you have impacted me just as much. That is the beauty of defining success around making an impact, because the impact is felt both ways. The transformation I saw in you in such a short time from the negative, self-absorbing guy that walked onto the range to this man ready to change the lives of those around him is truly a miracle. It is why I do what I do. I get to use the greatest individual game in the world to teach people about life, and there is one lesson I want to leave you with that wraps all this together."

"What is that, Caddie?"

"Every shot counts, Jack! If you look at life as a long round of golf, the similarities are remarkable. There are many great things about the game of golf, but perhaps the greatest is that truly every shot counts. From the first shot to the last, and all the good and bad ones between, every shot counts and influences your final score. No other sport is like that. The same is true in your life. Every relationship, every moment, and every decision count in your life. They are all equally important along the journey."

The caddie placed his hand on Jack's shoulder to let him know that this is where it all comes together and continued. "There will be blessings and there will be hardships, but be grateful for all of it! Don't expect the blessings; you aren't entitled to them, so appreciate them when they come. Hardships are often when one experiences the most personal development, so be grateful how you can use the hard times to grow. Every day alive is a gift, so be thankful for all of it and control what you can control. As I mentioned, every moment counts as well. From the big moments like the birth of a child or a new career decision, to the simple moments of a family dinner or casual sunset. Every moment matters, and you never know when a small moment will become significant. So be present and have enthusiasm for every moment.

"Every decision also counts and adds up through your round of life. When you decide to spend more quality time with your family, your overall relationships will grow. When you decide to eat a pint of ice cream every day, that also adds up to neglecting your overall health. Ice cream or occasionally working extra hours won't hurt your entire round, but they will certainly add up over time. Commit to your goals and having a foundation of balance and understand that every major or minor decision counts, so be consistent in your actions.

"You also need to trust that everything happens for a reason, even when you can't see it. We don't know how the dots will ultimately connect in our lives, but trust that the outside circumstances, daily moments, and personal decisions are all counting in your overall round. Once you have trust that the dots will ultimately connect, then you can freely make decisions that align with your values and live a life of integrity.

"Finally, when you create purposes that focus on positively impacting others instead of just yourself, the success of each impacted shot or relationship will be felt both inwardly and outwardly. Every relationship and personal interaction counts. You never know when or how big of an impact you can have on another life, but it is these compounding positive impacts on others that ultimately define the success of the round of your life. You will live a life of fulfillment and in turn realize who you are meant to be and why you are here. That's all it is, Jack!"

Jack, with tears in his eyes, reached out and hugged the caddie one last time. "Caddie, thank you again for the impact you just made in my life. I can't thank you enough, and I don't know if there is anything in the world to repay you to show you how much this has meant to me and changed my life when I most needed it."

"You can thank me by just remembering and living to make every shot count in your life, Jack!" With that, the caddie winked and handed Jack his clubs as he made his way back to the range to see what person he would be caddying for the next round in the afternoon.

Chapter 18

The Transformation

The sun was rising on another beautiful California summer morning. As the rays of pink and gold sprayed across the sky, there was no alarm clock ringing in Jack's house. Jack was already awake and sipping his coffee, ready to live and experience another day. As he sat outside watching the dark turn to light and going through his daily gratitude practice, he heard the pattering of footsteps as his kids made their way down the stairs. Jack smiled and made his way back inside the house.

"Another great day to enjoy life, kids! Who wants some eggs and pancakes?"

"Me!" exclaimed Will and Cassie at the same time. They were currently enjoying their summer break back home with their family.

As Jack started to whip up a good American breakfast, Patti made her way down the stairs.

"Smells like my favorite; now this is the man I married," said Patti as she smiled and approached Jack to give him a big morning hug and kiss.

The family gathered around the table for breakfast before the day's summer activities would take place.

"All right, you guys know the drill. What is everyone most looking forward to today? I think I know the answers with the big day ahead, but routine is routine."

"Well, Dad, I can't wait to have a day with Mom and get all pampered before our big trip this weekend. I always enjoy a summer spa day. Thanks for making the plans for us to do that to get ready for our vacation," said Cassie excitedly.

"What she said," laughed Patti, as she grabbed Jack's hand and looked deep into his eyes. She was just happy she recognized them again, and the look said enough.

"I think it looks like a beautiful day to hit the links, Pop. I can't wait to get out there and play with you and meet this Caddie you keep talking about. But get ready to finally lose, I almost have you," said Will with excitement. He was becoming a good golfer in his own right.

"You got it, fam! Let's get out there and have a great day."

With that, the girls made their way to the spa and the boys hopped into the car to make the hour drive south to San Diego. It had been about six months since Jack had played the course they were heading to, the same course where he had met the man who had changed his life forever. Jack wanted to check in with the caddie to share all the changes he had made to his life, as well as introduce his son to him and the course for their weekly round of golf together.

As Jack turned into the entrance, he couldn't help but think back to that special day and the profound impact the caddie had in helping Jack rediscover how to live a life of fulfillment. There were no grand goodbyes when the caddie left him after the eighteenth green, nor was there an exchange of each other's information. The moment had ended perfectly that day, and Jack did not want to disrupt that.

Jack started looking around anxiously with butterflies, the way people do when reconnecting with an old friend. Jack purposefully booked the first tee time on this Thursday morning again in hopes that the caddie would be out there working. He did not inform the clubhouse or ask anyone to pair him with the caddie as he wanted to make it a surprise. Jack walked past the driving range and into the clubhouse to check in and to see if his friend was working that day. He looked around the range and within the clubhouse, but there was no sight of the old man, so he approached the desk of the lone clubhouse pro in there.

"Hello, I am checking in for the Jack pairing at six thirty."

"Thank you, sir. Will you be riding or walking today?"

"Well, I thought you only allowed walking and required caddies from the last time I played."

"Interesting. No, you have the option for both here. Would you like to walk again?"

"Yes, that would be great. I also wanted to see if I could inquire about having the same caddie from last time pair with us this round again. Do you know what caddies are available?"

"There are a few young guys out back that can jump on your bags. Do you remember your caddie's name from last time?"

"He actually didn't give me his name last time. He just said he was an old-timer and everyone just called him Caddie. He was a man in his mid-sixties, calm presence about him and who knew the course like the back of his hand."

The young man slouched a bit, and Jack instantly got that bad feeling in the pit of his stomach. All of a sudden, his eagerness had evaporated and he didn't know if he wanted the man to answer.

"Yeah, you're talking about Jack the caddie. He was a longtime caddie here, so over time everyone just called him Caddie. Heck of a golfer too. That man had some stories. But unfortunately, he is no longer with us."

"No longer with you, like how? Like doesn't work here anymore?"

"No, he passed away. Just recently too, right after the start of the new year," the clubhouse pro said somberly. But as he started talking more about the caddie, his body language picked up remembering the fond memories of the man. "It is crazy too, he was caddying up until the very end of it. Caddie was diagnosed with a terminal illness about two years ago and was given two months to live. Our club tried to get him to retire, but he told management that he was going to make his remaining time in life count. He convinced them to let him work part-time, and for all he had done for the club, they felt obligated to let him live out his life doing what he loved. Things took a turn for the worse toward the end of the year last year. On the good days that he could physically make it out, he would come in and caddie just for free without even telling us sometimes. That man loved what he did, and it seemed that it was those hours out on the course that kept him going well past the end date they gave him."

Jack didn't know what to say. He had no idea the struggles or pain the caddie was going through that day, what ended up being one of his last days on earth. The caddie never once made it seem he was going through so much hardship or that his life was coming to an end. Jack had so much he wanted to say to the caddie. He wanted to reiterate his appreciation for the lessons he had taught him and was excited to tell him about how he had applied those principles and mindsets to better his life.

The pro sensed Jack's immense sadness and wanted to at least provide him some closure. "I do not know how well you knew the caddie, but it was incredible watching the impact he had not on just the people he caddied for daily but for this overall club in general. He was a special man and we set up a memorial for him on the first tee. He told us early on with his disease that once he passed, he wanted us to spread his ashes alongside the first tee box. He always said there is no feeling in the world like staring down the fairway on the first hole to start a round of golf. The whole round is in front of you and the possibilities, both the good and the bad, are endless. Thus, he wanted his ashes and that hope to be endless alongside the first tee. You have some space between you and the next tee time so take your time if you want to say goodbye."

Jack nodded and felt a little more peace in his heart as he knew the caddie had found his. With a smile, Jack reached out to shake the pro's hand and said, "Thank you for that and for letting me know. It must be hard for everyone who knew him. He really was a special man, and I am just lucky our lives crossed paths before he went. From the short time I knew him, that story and legacy to spread his ashes on the first tee makes complete sense and sounds very much like the caddie. It will carry extra meaning when we tee off today."

Jack looked over at his son and gave him a hug. The two made their way over to the first tee and found the mini memorial honoring the caddie. There was a big picture of him, bag in hand, with that big, contagious smiling, staring down the first tee. It mentioned his brief history moving out to California from the Midwest, his early amateur days as an elite golfer, and his long tenure at the club as first a golf pro and then a caddie. Below the picture and summary was a quote the caddie lived by:

"Golf to me is the greatest individual sport there is, because all the elements within a given round mirror a journey through life. There will be fairways and roughs, and there will be birdies and bogeys. But every stroke and situation are meaningful and add up to the overall score of your unique, individual round. The same is true in one's life. One lives a life full of fulfillment by not only understanding this but by doing and making every shot count!"

"He was a great man, son. I didn't know much about him, but the changes you've seen in my life are due to the principles and perspectives he shared with me when I was going through the tough times. While we enjoy the round of golf, I want to share some of those with you as well. Let me have a few minutes with him, so go hit some putts and we will tee off in five.

"Caddie, I wanted to have this conversation in person, and I've been thinking about what to say for some time now. I had no idea you were sick, but I am filled with gratitude that God kept you in this life for a little bit longer to fundamentally change mine. I was lost and had no idea how to find myself or what to do, until I met you. I know that all the dots connected for us to meet in that wonderful moment. Thank you, Caddie! I knew walking off the eighteenth green that the only way I could repay you was by living out the foundational principles and mindset mantras through everyday action. After some deep meditation, I made some major changes in my life. I made my family my priority and realized all the blessings I had. I went through gratitude exercises of writing to all those that had impacted my life, and you were the final one that I wanted to share that gratefulness with. I also committed to being in the moment with my family, like weekly rounds of golf with my son with no phone and maintaining more balance around my career. I did this by making major changes to my career. I have been in the sales game a long time, and I wanted to do something focused on others than myself. Thus, I met with my company and they created a role as a sales coach in helping mentor some of the new wave of talent coming in my company. It allowed me to refocus my energy and gave me the financial and personal flexibility I needed while also letting me give back and using my experiences to make an impact on my company and other sales professionals. I haven't felt this reinvigorated in years!"

Jack paused and realized one final lesson in that moment, almost as if the caddie was speaking to him. The caddie had used his passion and perspective to impact others using the game he revered and loved. He even did that until the very end, not letting his circumstances dictate his ability to stop making an impact. Here was an older-aged man in a relatively low-paying job dying from a terminal disease, and yet he was changing lives until his last breath. Jack thought to himself how you don't need to have high status or a certain type of income to positively change people's lives. Everyone has the ability to impact another using their gifts, and the beauty of life is you never know who that one person will be. The caddie's death wouldn't be celebrated in sports news outlets, but his legacy would continue to live on through the lives he touched. Jack laughed to himself and felt a quiet calm come about him as he had one final inspiration he wanted to share with the caddie as he knelt down and grasped the golf ball in his pocket that had led the two to come together.

"I can feel your presence with me, Caddie, or should I say . . . Jack. You never told me we shared the same name, but I guess that really wasn't your style. Thank you for inspiring me one last time. I love this game, and you helped me rediscover that. I remember the joy my father got from coaching young men, and I witnessed the impact you had on me teaching through the game of golf. I finally realize one of the reasons why I am here, to take the game I love and use it as my vehicle to positively impact young men the way you impacted me. I am going to get into coaching high school golf in any capacity. Not for the money, and not for the competition, but to give back to the game the way it has given to me through my father and yourself. I do not know why it took me this long to realize it, but that is the ultimate way to combine my passion and creating a purpose around making a positive impact. To steal from your line, I feel like I am standing on the first tee, looking down the fairway and feeling the excitement and nervousness of starting a new round. Only this time, I know from the first through the eighteenth hole to make every shot count!"

Jack stood up and found his son walking back up to the tee. The two grabbed their clubs and Jack joked, "The old one gets the honors," as he ran up to the tee box. But before Jack stepped up to his ball, he put his arm around his son while the two looked down the fairway, anticipating beginning the journey of another round.

"It is beautiful, isn't it? Be grateful every time you get to tee off and play another round of this great game, as you never know when it will be your last. A wise man once told me about this principle of gratitude . . ."

Acknowledgments

I would like to acknowledge the team that helped make this book a reality. When I first got the idea that I wanted to write *Every Shot Counts*, I did what everyone says not to do: think about the publishing process. I was concerned about do I have to get a literary agent? What if publishers don't like this book? Funny thing was, I didn't even have a book to share. I finally said, go for it, write and it will all come together. That was in 2019, and here we are in 2024 finally making it happen.

To the Big Idea to Bestseller team, thank you for making this happen. When I started to learn about self-publishing, it made it much easier to get over my fears and to get the book out there.

I knew nothing about self-publishing, so your guidance and expertise was critical in completing this milestone of publishing *Every Shot Counts*.

Jake Kelfer, founder of Big Idea to Bestseller, when our lives crossed paths more around basketball, who knew down the road that would lead to partnering together to publish my first-ever book. That is the beauty of life, you never know when the dots will connect. Appreciate your services and vision to help self-publishing authors accomplish their dreams.

Mikey Kershisnik, my author success coach, thank you for all you did to make this book publishing easy, fun, and a major success! Like any good project, you need someone on top of it to manage all the moving parts. I am so grateful for your leadership and attention to detail that made this book come to life.

David Caissie, my writing coach, thanks for all your feedback and coaching to dial in the framework of the story. As a first-time author, I didn't know what I didn't know, and to have your experience was a big part to creating the final framework.

Ashton Renshaw, my editor, thank you for all the final details that went into making a final edit become a book ready to be published. I know there were a lot of tweaks with being a first-time writer, so thank you for taking the time to ensure it would make a great experience for the readers.

Joey Graham, my longtime close friend, thank you for taking the time to provide feedback, suggestions, and moral support over the several years it took to make this book. Your connection to Jake led me to BIB and led to this launch. Love when life comes together like that!

About the Author

Kevin Donoher is a self-admitted sports addict that combined his passion for sports and writing to create personal development fables using lessons through sports as a metaphor to live a life of fulfillment. After five years of pursing his dream of coaching in collegiate basketball with several NCAA March Madness runs, his current day job consists of being a B2B Enterprise Account Executive working with large organizations to purchase software offerings that enable the way they interact with their end-customers. *Every Shot Counts* is his first personal development fable and hopes to make an impact on his readers in using the power of sports to transform our daily lives.

Kevin resides in Phoenix, Arizona, with his wife Sarah and their two young boys. When he isn't spending time going on family adventures with his active family or working on complex enterprise software sales, Kevin is working on improving his own golf game (major work in progress), training for an ambitious goal of completing an Ironman (another work in progress), and faithfully rooting on the San Francisco 49ers in hopes they can finally (after several brutal Super Bowl losses) win their sixth Lombardi Trophy.

9 781962 280624